Muezza
and Baby Jaan

Muezza and Baby Jaan

Stories from the Quran

Anita Nair

Illustrations by Harshad Marathe

PUFFIN BOOKS

PUFFIN BOOKS

USA | Canada | UK | Ireland | Australia
New Zealand | India | South Africa | China

Puffin Books is part of the Penguin Random House group of companies
whose addresses can be found at global.penguinrandomhouse.com

Published by Penguin Random House India Pvt. Ltd
7th Floor, Infinity Tower C, DLF Cyber City,
Gurgaon 122 002, Haryana, India

First published in Puffin Books by Penguin Random House India 2016

Text copyright © Anita Nair 2016
Illustrations copyright © Harshad Marathe 2016

ISBN 9780143333944

Book design and layout by Meena Rajasekaran
Printed at Replika Press Pvt. Ltd, India

www.penguinbooksindia.com

For
Chetan Krishnaswamy, who was there at the start when I sought direction and blessings, for spotting the crow pheasant and the possibilities,
and
Aarushi Chandel, my al-Zuhra—bright and constant star— who was there to see it through to the finish

Contents

Preface

It was 11 a.m. on 21 September 2013. I had just sat down with my pen and notebook. I had been working on my historical novel, *Idris*, when news came of unidentified gunmen opening fire in one of Nairobi's upscale malls. It was a Saturday and my first thought was for my friend Jayapriya Vasudevan, her husband, Harish Vasudevan, and her daughter, Miel Vasudevan, who were living in Nairobi. Where were they? Had they chosen to go to that mall on that particular day? Were they safe?

As soon as it was established that they were all right, I went back to my novel. Later in the day I began tracking the situation. TV channels and online newspapers had plenty to say. The mass shooting had left 67 people dead and more than 175 people injured.

Amidst all the kerfuffle of reportage, one thing struck me in particular. An eyewitness was reported to have said that the attackers had asked Muslims to leave, declaring that only non-Muslims would be targeted. Among other aspects of the vetting process, the hostages were asked to name Prophet Muhammad's mother as a litmus test that would distinguish Muslims from non-Muslims.

It seemed both astounding and horrific that a piece of information could have saved a life. But why was this information not out there for all to know?

In many parts of the world, including India, almost every non-Christian knows that Jesus's mother was Mary and his father, Joseph; and of the story of Jesus's birth and his crucifixion. Non-Hindus know that the Ramayana is about Rama and Sita and Rama's battle against Ravana; that the Mahabharata is about the Kauravas and the Pandavas, that Krishna was an avatar of Vishnu. But even the most erudite among non-Islamic people know nothing about the Quran or what is in it.

If you had asked me then what Prophet Muhammad's mother's name was, I would have stared back too, clueless.

Teaching a faith demands expertise; but what of the accompanying lore that goes into fleshing out the wisdom? Why is it that we barely know anything of Islamic lore? Religious preachers have always sought parables to explain a tenet. But even in isolation and removed from doctrine, these allegorical stories have an appeal of their own. The storyteller in me roused and shook herself.

Acts of terrorism perpetrated by Muslim fundamentalists had already made many non-Muslims wary of the religion. And I thought this was grossly unfair to Islam and what it taught. I had been brought up as a secular individual and felt a calling to clear this misinterpretation in my own way.

No religion preaches hate or violence. No religion condones killing or the taking of human life. However, flawed interpretations do lend a religion a misguided twist that it does not claim in the first place. Those with vested interests manipulate aspects of a religion to justify heinous crimes and the massacre of innocents. And so it had happened with Islam. And yet why was it that no one was actually trying to redeem the understanding of Islam? Why was no one willing to try and make Islam more accessible to the world so that the teachings in the Quran would be seen for what they truly are—a call to righteousness and peace—and not for what we have beguiled ourselves into believing?

During the writing of *Idris*, I had studied the Quran and tried to understand what I could of its lessons and the associated Islamic fables. But now I had another purpose. I had already written two books on mythology for children. One was based on Hindu mythology and the other drew on lesser-known world myths. I would now try and write about Islamic lore—stories culled from the Quran and the Hadith. And I was certain that the book had to be for children—for young minds are what we need to invest in for a chance of change. Let children everywhere—Hindu, Christian, Muslim, Jewish, Buddhist, Jain or otherwise—discover the stories from the Quran and delight in them and learn from them. Stories are, after all, stories; and no religion can stake claim to them.

In what could only be termed providential, I found a translation of a book of stories drawn from Ibn Kathir's *Al-Bidayah Wan-Nihayah* (The Beginning and the End). The author was born in AD 1300 and died in AD 1373. A Sunni scholar and historian of great repute, Ibn Kathir hailed from the Shafi'i school of Islamic law and lived during the reign of the Mamluk Sultanate in Syria.

Suddenly I knew where to begin. And then, as it usually happens with each book I write, two characters—a cat and a camel, in this case—appeared from nowhere, and I had my epiphany on how to take the book forward.

This is a book for young readers. But it is also a book for anyone who wonders what the Quran contains, apart from the teachings of a religion. In fact, al-Quran literally means 'the reading'; and how can a work that means this most beautiful of phrases be limited to just being a scripture? The wealth of its stories, and the lyricism, poetry and flow of its narrative make it as much a literary text as a holy book.

I have been told that I am entering dangerous territory. That, as a Hindu writing about the holy book of Islam, I'm inviting trouble. That to me smacks of prejudice more than anything else. How can any religion close its doors to someone who knows nothing of it? How does one learn about a religion unless one is given access to it?

And that is my only act of faith here. To lead from ignorance to the beginnings of knowledge; from prejudice to comprehension; and to reaffirm, in these times that are wreaked with discrimination and terror, that all religions are the same. That all religions just strive to make of us better human beings.

If only we would make an effort to understand their truth.

PS: The name of Prophet Muhammad's mother is Amina.

September 2016

1

Baby Jaan collapsed into a heap of sand at the foot of the date palm. She had had a busy evening, first revealing an oasis to a weary caravan and, just after the travellers had unloaded the camels and put up their tents, making the oasis disappear. *Phoosh!* With a wave of her hand, Baby Jaan had caused the illusion of the oasis to dissipate into just more dunes of sand.

The look of dismay on the men's faces and the tears in the women's eyes had made her giggle so hard that she'd begun whirling. Round and round till, as a whirlwind of sand, she had whirled away to another part of the desert. Only now, as she lay at the foot of the date palm as a little sand dune, she felt something akin to fear. Contrary to popular belief, djinns were prone to fear, too. And she was, after all, only a baby djinn.

Baby Jaan's parents had left her at home to go on a raiding mission against the most vicious of djinns, the Guls. She had been told to stay at home and practise her shape-shifting. 'Any self-respecting Jaan should be able to take at least a thousand and one shapes,' Abby Jaan had said as he'd changed from a horse to a waterskin to a tree to a sword in the blink of an eye.

Umm Jaan had turned into a mop and wiped clean the wooden table they'd had their dinner on. The wooden table had then stood upright. It was their servant, whose job was to be table, chair, bed or sometimes a stick. 'You must be able to shift your shape to anything you need to be. That's the secret of being a good Jaan. Or in our battle against the Guls, we will lose,' Umm Jaan had said as she'd beaten the carpet that was a real carpet with their servant who was now a stick.

Baby Jaan had kept at it for a few hours but she was soon bored, and that's when she'd spotted the caravan trudging through the dunes. It had been such delicious fun to mislead them . . . but where on earth was she now? And what if there were Guls nearby? She would be just a little chicken bone to them! To snap with their fang-like teeth and lick out the marrow with their long, curling tongues.

A small sob escaped her. *Umm . . . Abby . . . where are you?*

Muezza sat amidst the crown of leaves on top of the date palm and prodded its soft heart with his claws. *Could there be a stupider cat than him in the whole universe including the seven heavens,* he asked himself, slapping his forehead with his paw.

As always, he had been sitting in the saddle along with his Shahir as they rode through the desert. Shahir and his followers had stopped to rest at an oasis when Muezza had decided to stretch his legs.

Spotting something move in the sand, Muezza had narrowed his eyes. A snake of the desert! *Aha,* Muezza had thought as he'd padded his way through the sand. But the snake had been wilier and quicker than he had expected it to be. One moment it was slithering through the sand and the next minute it was gone. That was when Muezza had seen the date palm. A little away from the oasis and standing like a sentinel of the vast desert.

Muezza had decided that he would climb the date palm. From there he would have a vantage point of the snake's whereabouts. For a while he had sat there examining every ripple and crease in the sand, but soon the warmth of the sun and the rather cosy perch he had found had made him sleepy. And then disaster had struck: Muezza fell asleep. When he woke up hearing sounds in the distance, he saw, to his horror, Shahir saddle up his horse and leave without him! How could it be that his Shahir had forsaken him? And then Muezza had consoled himself that his Shahir would come back for him.

For when Shahir—that was Muezza's name for him—would call for Muezza and realize that he was missing, Shahir would surely come looking for him, calling out, 'Muezza, Muezza, where are you?' Until then, Muezza would wait atop the date palm.

Suddenly, down below, Muezza saw movement in the sand. The snake *was* there. God, the most merciful, had made sure that Muezza wouldn't go hungry. Tonight Muezza would have snake for dinner! Snakes could be chewy, but he had nothing much to do till his Shahir came for him. So snake it would be!

'Ouch!' Baby Jaan hollered as something landed on her middle—or what must have been her middle. For how could a heap of sand have a middle? But that was neither here nor there, she thought, as the weight refused to budge and until it did, Baby Jaan was stuck. 'Get away from me!' she screamed.

Now, Jaans have a voice like wind through a reed, whistling sharp and quite mellifluous if one likes pipe music and that sort of thing. But to Muezza, it sounded like a silly, petrified mouse. And so he dug into the sand with greater fervour.

'Stop it! You're hurting me,' Baby Jaan cried. 'I am not a mouse for you to pounce on!'

Muezza paused, unable to believe his ears. How could a pile of sand speak? But it had to be the pile of sand, for there was nothing else there! Neither snake nor mouse. He stopped digging and said quite firmly, 'I will have you know that I don't scare. Besides, I am protected. So you better tell me what idiotic game you think this is! But first, reveal who you are.'

'For a cat, you use big words,' Baby Jaan said. 'You see, if you don't move, I can't shift my shape!'

Muezza stepped back. The pile of sand he had been standing on became a little fountain. 'What on earth?' he spat as a jet of water hit him on his nose.

Baby Jaan giggled and the water jet shimmered with the force of her merriment. 'I can be whatever I want to be,' she said. She was still working on her shape-shifts, but the cat didn't have to know that.

'Well, I don't like this,' Muezza hissed. 'And I can pounce on a fountain, too!'

Baby Jaan's mouth opened round as a moon. The water jet turned into a

circle of water, but Muezza didn't seem to notice and neither did Baby Jaan. Only very experienced Jaans managed to accomplish this. And here was Baby Jaan doing it as if it were the easiest thing.

'Tell you what,' she said hastily. 'Usually Jaans take the form of a white camel in the desert. I could be that!'

Muezza shrugged. A camel was a camel. White or beige. Single-humped or double-humped. So he stretched and yawned, feigning nonchalance, as Baby Jaan prepared to become a white camel. But Muezza's jaw almost fell open at the transformation. She *was* now a baby camel—and white, too. He had seen nothing like it ever before. He put a paw under his jaw and pushed his mouth shut. The camel kneeled on the sand.

'You don't need to bow to me. I am not Shahir. Just his cat.'

Baby Jaan stared. 'I wasn't bowing to you, silly cat. I was just preparing to sit. But tell me, what are you doing in the desert?' she asked curiously.

'Waiting for my Shahir to come find me,' Muezza said, peering at the horizon.

'Who is this Shahir you speak of?' she asked.

Muezza sat up. 'He has ninety-nine names. Shahir is just one of them. It means well known.'

The white camel blinked. The silence of the dusk was broken only by a loud rumble from the camel's belly. 'Oops . . . that means I'm hungry!' Baby Jaan said, lifting a camel lip to reveal gigantic teeth. Umm Jaan always made sure that Baby Jaan was fed every eight hours.

Night fell suddenly as it does in the desert. Stars appeared in the skies. Countless stars, some of which Muezza had learnt to identify while sitting on his Shahir's lap. But right now, Muezza was more struck by the hungry rumble from Baby Jaan's belly. Who knew what djinns liked to eat? If they found nothing, then maybe a djinn wouldn't turn up its nose at a cat. Especially a well-fed, much-cherished cat like him.

'It is said that anyone who recites Shahir's ninety-nine names once during the day and once at night will never be stricken with afflictions,' Muezza said, hoping to deflect the djinn's thoughts away from food.

'What do *you* like to eat?' Baby Jaan asked anyway.

Muezza ignored the question and continued, 'And if you were to recite them twelve times after the nightly prayer, it is said that Shahir himself will lead you to *jannat*! That, white camel, means paradise. Do you know what paradise is?

'Paradise has rivers of water, whose taste and smell never changes. It has rivers of milk, whose taste also remains unchanged. It has rivers of wine that is delicious to those who drink from it, as well as rivers of clear, pure honey. Everyone reclines on raised thrones, and it is neither hot nor cold as in paradise there is no sun and no moon.'

Muezza wondered if he should tell Baby Jaan that everyone rides white camels in jannat. But he wasn't sure she would like it. So he shoved that thought aside and went on. 'Vessels of silver and cups of crystal are passed around; everyone's garments are made of fine green silk embroidered with gold. All are adorned with bracelets of silver. There are houris with wide, lovely eyes.'

'Stop, cat,' Baby Jaan said, batting her eyelids. 'Do you think I would make a good houri?'

Muezza shuddered at the thought of Baby Jaan as a houri. But, hiding his emotions, he persisted, 'No one can hear any vain or sinful speech but only the peaceful greeting of "Salaam, Salaam". There is always shade, and bunches of fruit hang low within reach. One can have fruit from whichever tree they choose, and the flesh of fowls that they desire.'

'Enough, cat, enough. Don't talk about food! You're making me hungrier than I can bear to be.' Baby Jaan frowned. 'Are you sure you're not a Jaan who has shape-shifted to a cat? You know way too much to be just a cat.'

'I am not just any cat. I am Muezza, Shahir's favourite cat. And what I know about Shahir's teachings, even the sahabahs may not know as much!'

Muezza saw that what he said had made no impact at all on the baby camel, whose teeth seemed to grow larger by the minute. *What was he going to do?* And then he had a thought. A brilliant I-amaze-myself sort of idea.

'Would you like to hear a story, white camel?' Muezza hoped that by the time he would finish the story, his Shahir would've come to his rescue.

'Call me Baby Jaan. That's my name,' she said, leaning on the date palm and scratching her back against it. 'I like stories. Especially stories with happy endings.'

'In that case,' said Muezza, arranging his body so the desert chill wouldn't seep into his bones, 'let me begin with mine. It is not necessary for a storyteller to reveal who he is or what makes him a storyteller. But as God, the most merciful, knows, my life may have been that of an ordinary cat's. Had my Shahir not taken me into his home and heart, and made my life quite extraordinary.'

2

'Long, long ago . . . actually no one knows how long ago—in fact, long before the time of my Shahir—there lived a man like no other. His name was Nuh.

'It was a strange time they lived in. Nothing was like we know it now,' Muezza said, peering into Baby Jaan's eyes to see if they had grown heavy with sleep. 'Are you awake, Baby Jaan, or am I telling the story to the stars and the sand?'

Baby Jaan turned around and snorted. A long, deep snort that hurled Muezza many inches away.

'Careful!' he shrieked. 'You have no idea how strong you are!' And in his head he screamed, *you silly-moronic-idiotic-nincompoopish-foolish-booby-blockhead-imbecile baby camel!*

Muezza padded back to his warm place in the sand and snuggled against her side.

'Go on . . .' Baby Jaan said in a small voice.

'In those days, people worshipped idols made of stone. A false set of idols with the strangest of names, if you please. Wadd, Suwa', Yaghuth, Ya'uq, Nasr . . . ever heard of anything like that?' Muezza asked, beginning to enjoy himself. It had never occurred to Muezza that telling a story could give as much pleasure as listening to one!

Baby Jaan shook her head. How could any cat, even a silly, fat cat like Muezza, know so much? She wondered if Abby Jaan or Umm Jaan knew half as much as Muezza did.

'Now, tell me who is God?' Muezza asked suddenly. Shahir often punctuated his sermons with questions and Muezza was merely following his master.

Baby Jaan shook her head. 'God' was a word she didn't know. So how could she answer?

'No wonder you djinn lot are the way you are!' Muezza said with as much scorn as he could muster.

Baby Jaan felt a great sob grow in her. No one—but no one—had ever spoken to her like this. Then the sob turned into anger. And without her knowledge, Baby Jaan began shifting shape. A spark flew. Then another. Then a lick of flame! The camel was turning into fire by the time Muezza wised up.

'Baby Jaan, listen!' he said hastily. 'You are going to love this story.'

The sparks disappeared and Baby Jaan took a deep breath to snuff the rage out. Then she counted till ten under her breath. The truth was, she could only count till ten. And that's what Umm Jaan would say to Abby Jaan when he'd get angry. *Count till ten and you will calm down.* And lo, Baby Jaan did actually feel calm.

'Where was I?' Muezza asked, stretching his back.

A spark flew up to the night sky. Muezza hissed in fright. Then pulling himself together, he began the story again.

God saw that since the time Adam was sent to earth, much had changed. Ten generations had passed and God's words were no longer respected or even followed. Iblis, God's enemy, had worked his way into the hearts of people; no one knew the difference between good and evil, and neither did they care. Among his people, Nuh alone knew that they needed to change. So God chose Nuh to be His prophet and asked him to preach the word of God to the people. Nuh was a fine orator, and he told everyone stories about the mysteries of life and the wonders of the universe. He described how the day is born, which is when things are grown, and how the night follows, which is the time to rest. He spoke of God, the divine creator and of the beauty of the earth. But no one listened to or even acknowledged his stories! They were too busy amassing wealth instead of wisdom. Only the poor and the weak found solace in his words. In fact, when Nuh began to speak of the punishment that awaited the people who forgot God, the rich and mighty became resentful and angry.

But Nuh persisted even though his people were a cursed lot. They jeered at Nuh and mocked him and his attempts to make them give up their evil ways. He did his best; when they shouted at him to stop his silly sermons, Nuh shouted out the message of God even louder.

Eventually a small group of people came to Nuh and began following God's path. But everyone else continued as they had always done. Think of anything that was evil and they did just that.

'Well, you call yourself a prophet, but we see you and we see just a man. And look at the motley lot who follow you . . . all beggars and the infirm . . . fools and the forlorn . . . Actually, come to think of it, there is nothing exceptional about you either. In fact, if this is the best your god can do, he can't be much of a god,' one of them snarled, vexed with Nuh's attempts to reform him. 'Get away from me, you liar!'

'GET AWAY, YOU LIAR!' the crowd took up the chant.

'How much do you get paid to mouth these lies? We'll give you more to shut up!' a heckler called out to Nuh, who was standing at the street corner, undaunted by the mob.

'Listen, listen, my people,' Nuh said, trying to outshout them. 'I want nothing from you; neither wealth nor power. My reward is God!'

An old woman leaning on her stick tottered towards him. She held the palm of her hand to her brow to shade her eyes from the bright light of the morning sun and peered at him. Then she cackled, 'I have been hearing plenty about you, Nuh. But you are just a man trying to make yourself important. If God wanted to send a messenger to earth, why was an angel not sent?'

The old woman's son, who was one of the chiefs of the land, came towards his mother and pushed her away. 'Go home, old one!' he hollered and, turning towards Nuh—who was trying to help the old woman to her feet, he thundered, 'As for you, ask your god to show us what he is capable of.'

Nuh shook his head in grief. 'What have you said, my brother? You do not know what you are saying . . .'

Later that evening, as Nuh said his prayers, he pleaded with God to intervene. The disbelievers were only growing in number and getting wickeder by the day.

And God spoke to Nuh, telling him what must be done.

So the prophet and his small band of followers went to the mountains and cut down old cypress trees. Then they carried the sawed-off planks to the highest point in the land and set about building an ark. God had decreed its size and shape and everything else that was to be done.

The people walking past laughed at Nuh. Only a madman would build a ship so far from the sea! 'And you want us to believe that you are God's messenger,' they said to him, pelting the ark with stones, rotten eggs, overripe tomatoes and peaches gone bad. When the ark was finished, God asked Nuh to cover the planks and the keel with pitch.

It was a hot summer day, and the earth and skies were parched. 'Why is God asking us to cover the ark with a waterproofing substance?' someone asked.

Nuh shrugged. 'God must have a reason to do so!'

When all of it was accomplished, God spoke to Nuh again. 'Lead into the ark your family and all who believe in me. Then you must bring into the ark pairs of every living creature, a male and a female of each animal, bird, reptile, insect and beetle. After that you must raise the gangplank to the deck and unfurl the sail and be prepared for what will come next.'

The people watched as creature after creature—kangaroo and zebra, ox and elephant, horse and anteater, butterfly and snail, tortoise and alligator, ibis and crow, swan and heron—clambered aboard the ark.

One last time, Nuh decided to try and convince the people to place their faith in God, but when he went to them, they stuck their fingers in their ears and pulled their robes over their heads and screamed abuses at him.

Nuh stood with his head bowed before the ark that evening. God would bring down punishment on this ungodly lot, he knew it.

That night a wind began to blow. A hard, howling wind that made houses creak and trees shake. The stars disappeared and a pitch-like darkness descended. Then it began to rain. And as the rain fell, cataracts gushed on earth. Lakes, reservoirs and canals began to spill over. Rivers swelled and

wells filled up. Neither the wind nor the rain stopped, and the waters began to flood the land.

People ran from their waterlogged homes and sought the highest trees to climb on to. One of Nuh's sons, who thought his father a silly old fool, ran this way and that, seeking refuge. Nuh called to him from the ark, 'Come, my son. Join us. God will take care of us!'

But the boy wouldn't listen. He saw the wind billowing the sail, and tossing and rocking the ark. It looked as though the ship would soon topple and sink! 'Are you mad?' he called out. 'I am going to climb the highest mountain and stay there.'

But as the waters rose, even the highest mountaintop was swallowed. Only the ark stayed afloat and all who were on it knew they were under God's protection.

The wind and the rain continued, and no one on the ark could make out whether it was night or day, whether they were on land or at sea. All around was just water, giant waves slapping against the ark with a ferocity that made their blood congeal like gum. Yet God's fury was still unabated.

Finally one day, the rains ceased and the winds pushed the ark to the summit of Mount Judi. And there the ark would stay till the great floods receded.

'And before you ask me why Mount Judi,' Muezza said, 'I'll tell you the reason for that as well.'

'It is said that when God had decided to send Nuh to spread His word, He had told the mountains, "I want to make my servant Nuh rest on one of you."

'All the mountains had vied with one another to tell God how perfect they were to offer sanctuary to Nuh and the ark—except for Mount Judi in

Mosul. Mount Judi had remained quiet and modest, and had said, "I am not worthy of Nuh's Ark berthing upon me."

'God had looked at Mount Judi and smiled. Humility is a virtue that allows a being to improve and so God had decreed the ark to halt at Mount Judi.

'And when the ship came to the mountain and nudged it, it trembled, overwhelmed with apprehension. The people and animals on board screamed in fright. Hearing the wailing and the yowling, Nuh peered out of a window of the ark and called out, "My Lord! Steady the boat!"'

3

Baby Jaan's eyes had popped out of her head. A sea as vast as the desert they were in and only water on all sides! It must have been most frightening, she thought, snuggling closer to Muezza. Thank heavens, she was not alone in the desert! Atleast they had each other.

'What happened then? You said you were going to tell me about yourself?' she asked softly. Muezza seemed lost in a world of his own.

He shook his head to clear it. The thought of all that water had left him tongue-tied as well. Then he continued with his story.

The ark stayed on top of Mount Judi for many days. Nothing moved. Only the wind stirred. The waves beat against the ark, and that was the only sound. Everyone walked around on tiptoe, afraid that the smallest sound would cause something to happen.

One day, Nuh noticed a crack in the ark. He wondered how it could have happened. A crack on the side of a ship was a dangerous thing—once water got in, nothing could be done. The ark would sink. So he repaired the crack quickly.

What Nuh didn't know was that Iblis, God's enemy, had entered the ark as a wild boar. While all other creatures on board slept at night, the wild boar wandered through the ark. It mucked the place with filth, and slammed its tusks on the wooden sides, forming gouges.

Every day Nuh had to clean and repair the ship. One day, the chisel slipped from his hand and cut his thumb. As drops of blood fell on to the deck, God caused a lion to appear from them.

That night the lion stood guard. When Iblis, in the form of the wild boar, set about ruining all of Nuh's work done during the day, the lion growled. The wild boar fled, petrified at the sight of the lion. But the boar was cunning as cunning could be, and so he sneezed. Out dropped a rat, which began gnawing and chewing on the boards of the ship. For a while, the lion only stared at the rat, growling softly.

Muezza stopped abruptly and, leaning towards Baby Jaan, he asked in a theatrical whisper, 'What do you think happened then?'

'The lion chased the rat!' she answered, jumping to her feet in excitement.

'Lions don't chase rats!' said Muezza, blowing at his whiskers. 'The lion sneezed—'

'And so the rat flew overboard!' Baby Jaan interrupted gleefully.

'Nope! By the way, am I telling the story or are you?' He frowned. Really, this Baby Jaan was getting ahead of herself.

'Sorry . . .' Baby Jaan said in a small voice that sounded like a tiny rat-squeak. It set Muezza's teeth on edge.

'So, anyway, the lion sneezed and out came a cat! A cat like me! Handsome, strong and a fighter!' Muezza preened.

'And . . .?'

'And the cat did what cats do! Pounced on the rat and killed it. That was the end of Iblis on that ship. And thereafter cats have always been around. So you see, Baby Jaan, cats go back a long way . . .'

Baby Jaan looked fixedly at Muezza. How wonderful it must be to be Muezza, she thought.

'Muezza,' she said, 'what about camels? How did they appear?'

He yawned. 'It's been a long day and a long story. Don't I get to nap? Just a catnap . . .' he pleaded.

'Go to sleep. I'll watch over you,' she said. 'But when you wake up, I want my camel story!'

'Agreed!' Muezza said, curling up into a ball.

Baby Jaan smiled. Muezza thought his heart must have stopped in fright. Camels shouldn't smile, he decided.

4

Muezza woke up with a start. Where was Baby Jaan? The baby camel seemed to have disappeared. Just then, he thought he heard a breath exhaled in the distance. Had his Shahir returned? He uncurled himself and was about to meow to announce his pleasure and presence when a frond of date palm whispered, 'Don't make a sound. A Pali is out!'

Muezza froze. He had heard of the Pali, a strange sort of djinn with a forked black tongue. It went about licking the feet of man and beast, draining their blood with each lick.

'What do I do, Baby Jaan?' Muezza whispered as softly as he could.

'Dig a hole in the sand and crouch inside it. I will cover you,' Baby Jaan whispered back. 'Hurry up, there is no time to lose!'

Muezza burrowed into the sand and peered through the fronds of the palm leaf at the shadow that was drawing closer. The whistling dark shape loomed near and flitted by. Then it paused for a moment and turned. Then it flew back again and hovered over the spot where Baby Jaan and Muezza were, its forked black tongue flicking out into the air, searching for a whiff of life.

Muezza shut his eyes tight and held his breath. *Go away, Pali, go away*, he whispered to himself.

'You can open your eyes and come out of the sand now.' Baby Jaan's voice broke through the silence.

Muezza dug himself out of the sand and stretched. 'Whew!' he said. 'That was close!'

'Indeed, it was . . .' Baby Jaan said. She had become a camel again, Muezza saw with great relief. It had been eerie to hear a palm leaf speak.

'But I must confess that Palis are dimwits! Not vicious or cunning like a

Gul, Marid or Si'lat. If it had been one of them, you would have been just bone and gristle by now!'

Muezza shuddered and crept closer to Baby Jaan, who seemed to know a lot about the various djinns.

Baby Jaan continued. 'Umm Jaan—that's my mother—says it is quite possible to fool the Pali. If two people lie end to end with the soles of their feet touching, the Pali goes away thinking that it's a strange creature with two heads!'

'Like an earthworm. That's a creature with two heads,' Muezza said, peering up at the skies to see if dawn was approaching.

'Well, since you're awake, why don't you tell me the story about the camel?' Baby Jaan asked.

'Now?'

'What's wrong with now?' she bristled. 'You really are an ungrateful cat. I saved your life, didn't I?'

Muezza felt ashamed at his own churlishness. 'Sorry, sorry, sorry, Baby Jaan!' Muezza said. 'Of course I will tell you the story . . . but I must warn you that the story isn't like the story of my genesis.'

'Genesis?' Baby Jaan frowned. 'Why do you need to use such big words?'

'The story of my birth, then. So listen. God, in His wisdom, decided to create man. So He took a ball of clay and began moulding one out of it. He made a torso and limbs; He fashioned a face and all that fills a man. Then He breathed life into the clay and gave it a name. Adam.

'Now, when God created Adam, He had taken a little more clay than He needed. So with what was left over He shaped a creature that was totally unlike a man. But it, too, had a torso and limbs, a neck and a face. And there still remained a bit of clay. So He pressed the bit on to the back of the creature. And so—'

'And so the camel was created!' Baby Jaan squealed in excitement. 'So man is actually my cousin, Muezza. Did you realize that?'

He swallowed. To call a man a camel was an insult, he knew. But maybe Baby Jaan was right. Some people did indeed behave like bad-tempered camels.

Muezza sighed. He was tired and sleepy. He thought of his cushion in Shahir's home. A golden-yellow cushion with a fringe. So if he was bored, he could worry it as if it were a rat's tail. A cushion so soft that each time he sank into it, he never wanted to rise and stretch again.

Baby Jaan yawned. A yawn that seemed to begin at the tip of her tail, it made her mouth seem so big and cavernous that Muezza almost yowled in fright. For a baby camel, she had a rather big yawn.

'I have a question,' Baby Jaan said.

Muezza rolled his eyes. It was indeed a strange time that djinns—or camels—had started asking questions. A cat may. In fact, a cat may even look at a queen, he had heard. But right now he was at this creature's mercy, and he had to answer questions even if they were silly and idiotic.

That was what he had learnt from his Shahir. Once, after Shahir had finished preaching, a man in the audience had raised his hand. Shahir had smiled and waved for him to speak. Everyone had turned curiously to see who the man was and what his question would be. Even Muezza, who by then had known to the last syllable the questions that would pop up once Shahir had spoken the word of God.

The man in the crowd was tall and bulky, and his skin was wrinkled like well-worn leather. His eyes were sharp and piercing, and his voice—when he'd spoken—was like a thunderclap.

'How old are you?'

The audience had burst into laughter. Even Muezza had felt a smile grow on his face.

'I am sixty-two,' Shahir had said.

The man had waited expectantly. He'd had a strange smile on his face. 'How old are you?' he'd asked again.

Shahir had stared at him for a moment. Then he'd smiled. 'I am twenty-two,' he'd said.

The crowd had tittered. 'Shut up and sit down!' someone had hollered.

When the crowd had all left, one of Shahir's followers had said, 'Those madmen . . . I'm glad you put him in his place.'

Shahir had shaken his head. 'But his question was a real one.'

'Asking you how old you are?'

'Yes,' Shahir had said, 'he was asking me when Angel Jibril first appeared before me. I am not the man I was prior to that. So, I am but twenty-two.'

Muezza blinked, wondering what Baby Jaan's question would be. A cat's blink that could say so much without saying anything at all. 'Ask away,' he told Baby Jaan.

Baby Jaan frowned. 'The thing is, I don't entirely believe your story.'

'What story?' Muezza asked. Didn't the camel realize that Muezza had narrated more than one? Silly, silly camel.

'The one about Adam and I being cousins,' she said, trying to scratch behind her ear with her foreleg.

'What are you doing, Baby Jaan?'

'I need to scratch behind my ear,' said Baby Jaan.

'What a silly creature you are!' Muezza said. 'Use your hind leg. Not your front one. Do I have to teach you how to scratch behind your ear?'

Baby Jaan—who had been wondering how she was going to get to that itchy spot behind her ear and how hard it was to be a camel—smiled. And Muezza thought that he was beginning to quite like her smiles.

'And for your information, I didn't say man and you are cousins,' Muezza protested.

'Didn't you? I thought you did,' Baby Jaan said, licking her hooves.

'*What are you doing?*' Muezza asked again, now shaking his head. Was this camel mad? He looked at the sky. The moon wasn't full. So it couldn't be moonstroke . . .

MUEZZA AND BABY JAAN 27

'I'm grooming myself like you were doing,' Baby Jaan said.

Muezza struck his paw on his head. He didn't know whether to laugh or cry. 'Baby Jaan,' he said, 'camels don't groom themselves like cats do! We are different.'

'Oh,' said Baby Jaan. Her mouth was full of sand from her hooves by then and she was wondering what she had been doing wrong.

'So why is it that you don't believe my story?' Muezza asked, remembering to be affronted. Cats were not really confrontational; cats walked away. Or at least he did. But he wasn't going to let a wet-behind-the-ears camel question his story.

Baby Jaan now sat on her haunches. But Muezza was too annoyed to comment.

'If God made Adam from clay, why is it that there are many-coloured men?' Baby Jaan pulled a corner of her mouth sideways into a smirk.

Muezza's jaw almost dropped. But he put on a bored expression that he could produce with little effort.

'What do you mean?'

'Just yesterday, when I was wandering through the desert, I saw four kinds at least. Black, brown, yellow and white. So that's my question. What clay changes colour like that?'

Muezza smiled. It was the sort of smile he had seen fathers use when their sons asked them complicated questions about simple phenomena, like where the sun goes to sleep or if the throat hurts when one's voice breaks.

'Ah,' he purred, 'I gave you the abridged version . . .'

'Abridged?' Baby Jaan's eyes were as big as tajines. 'Where's the bridge? When did you cross it?'

Muezza took a deep breath. 'Abridged means the twenty-second-long version instead of the sixty-minute-long one.'

'Oh, in that case, may I have the sixty-minute-long version?' Baby Jaan requested, settling into a position that was more natural for a camel.

'Yes, you may,' Muezza said with a wave of his hand.

There was something addictive about this storytelling business, Muezza decided as he gazed at the skies for an opening phrase.

'And this Adam—didn't you say Nuh came ten generations after Adam? But why did God create Adam in the first place?' Baby Jaan asked, suddenly struck by the thought. 'You have to tell me that as well!'

'You sound like the angels.' Muezza shook his head. 'They asked God the same question!'

'Great minds think alike . . .' Baby Jaan said airily. She had heard one of her uncles say this and had been waiting to use it.

'And fools seldom differ . . .' Muezza retorted. 'But that isn't the point. Listen to the story.'

5

One day, God called His angels and said, 'I am going to introduce generations after generations of mankind on earth.'

The angels were not pleased at all. They looked at each other and then protested all in one voice. 'Why would you want to put on earth creatures that will make mischief and, worse, spill blood? If you need to place someone there, you have us—those who worship you.'

God peered at His angels and said quietly, 'I know what you don't.'

The angels didn't know what to say and so they did as God asked them to. They went to different corners of the earth and brought back soil that was red, white, brown and black; soil that was soft and malleable, soil that was hard and gritty. It came from mountains and valleys, riverbeds and estuaries, deserts and plains, from deep inside a cave and from the seashore. Soil that was both arid and fertile.

And God took all of the soil and mixed it with water, which was left to stand till the water was mostly absorbed and what was left was a sticky mud. That was left to stand again, till it began to smell and the colour turned darker. This was black, smooth clay. Like the sounding clay used by the potter, when it was dry, it made a ringing sound if one tapped it.

It is from this that God made man. He then left the soulless body to dry.

'So I'm just all clay?' Baby Jaan's mouth trembled.

Muezza smiled. 'You are and you are not. For you are a djinn. And djinns are born of smokeless fire.'

'That's true.' She smiled, her eyes lighting up.

'But how did the clay come alive?'

'When God breathed into it.'

'So I have God's breath in me!' Baby Jaan gleamed like al-Zuhra in the sky.

'You look like the brightest star in the sky,' Muezza said. 'The morning star!'

'Wouldn't *you* if you found out you have God's breath in you?' Baby Jaan asked.

'But I do!' he said. 'All of God's creatures have God's breath, Baby Jaan.'

'That means you and I are cousins!'

Muezza smiled. She was such a child, he thought.

'I wonder what's keeping my Shahir,' he said suddenly.

Baby Jaan's face fell. 'Oh,' she said.

She looked away, towards the horizon. The thought of Muezza going away left a hole where her heart ought to have been; and a fearful heat of trepidation spread through her belly. She felt her eyes fill up.

The skies were changing colour. The night withdrew even as the sun rose.

'There he is,' Muezza said, stretching.

Baby Jaan tried to do the same and stopped abruptly. 'What do you mean? Who is here?'

Muezza rolled his eyes. 'The guardian of the day. The sun, you *ablah* camel!'

Baby Jaan grinned. She didn't mind being called stupid. In fact, she was so relieved. For a moment her heart had stopped. She had thought Muezza's Shahir had returned.

'We can go look for some food now,' Muezza said.

'But where do we find food?' asked Baby Jaan.

Muezza clambered up the date palm. Then he scampered back down and said, 'I can see the oasis I wandered away from at some distance. Let's go there.'

Baby Jaan nodded. 'Hop on to my back,' she said.

'You don't mind?' Muezza asked, surprised. He had planned to walk alongside Baby Jaan.

'Of course not . . . I wouldn't ask if I did.'

Baby Jaan grinned and lowered herself by kneeling on her forelegs. Muezza leapt on to her back, quite glad for the ride. His paws were not really built for desert trekking.

'I'm happy I have you as navigator,' Baby Jaan said as they neared the oasis.

Muezza shrugged. He had learnt the art of being a lookout while perched on Shahir's horse. He had always thought of it as a simple enough thing but it was nice to be appreciated. Praised even.

6

The oasis was quiet. There wasn't anyone there. Muezza jumped down from Baby Jaan's back.

'Where are you going?' she cried out.

But Muezza shot away like a streak of lightning across the dappled ground of the oasis. When he came back, he had a piece of meat in his mouth. He dropped it near Baby Jaan.

'Breakfast for the lady,' he said with a neat little bow.

'But I don't eat meat,' Baby Jaan said in a small voice.

'Are you a vegetarian?' Muezza, who was looking for a comfortable spot to have a little snooze, frowned. Whoever heard of a vegetarian djinn?

'Camels are vegetarian,' Baby Jaan snorted. 'But if I'm really hungry, I'll eat anything.'

'Like what?'

'Like thorns, bones, meat—even a tent if there is one around!' Baby Jaan exclaimed.

'Oh,' Muezza said, turning pale. Or as pale as a cat could get.

'I think the world is omnivore,' Baby Jaan added, quite oblivious to Muezza's unease.

'For a baby camel, you know big words . . .' Muezza said slowly, climbing a date palm. What if she decided that she would like to snack on a cat?

'It's a djinn trait.' Baby Jaan fluttered her eyelashes.

'Why don't you turn into another creature for a bit and eat the meat?' Muezza asked, settling down on the crown of leaves.

'What should I be?'

'Well, if you turn into a rat or a newt, I will feel obliged to kill you,' Muezza said thoughtfully.

'If I turn into a dog, I would feel obliged to chase you!' Baby Jaan retorted.

'Tell you what, stay a camel . . . I think there is some camel food stored somewhere here,' Muezza said, climbing down.

'I need to drink some water first,' Baby Jaan said. And walking to the pool, she began drinking deeply.

For several minutes, Muezza watched in astonishment as Baby Jaan drank up what seemed to be one-tenth of what was a rather large pool!

'Stop!' he said loudly. 'You're going to burst!'

'Not yet,' she replied, walking back to where Muezza lay curled.

'Tell you what,' she teased Muezza, grinning at his expression, 'now I'm really hungry.' She paused. 'Very, very hungry.'

Muezza didn't want to scramble up the date palm this time. To be afraid of a camel seemed almost a little offensive to a cat such as he. And yet his muscles clenched.

Baby Jaan burst into a giggle. 'Gotcha!'

'What?' Muezza asked. A cat doesn't take kindly to being mocked.

'I'm very hungry for a story!' Baby Jaan said, crouching next to Muezza.

'Iblis!' Muezza muttered.

'This Iblis . . . who is he? You mentioned him once as God's enemy. Tell me, tell me . . .' Baby Jaan chanted.

'Hmm . . . which means I will have to go back to the story of your cousin.'

'*Who?*' Baby Jaan asked, her mouth fully open.

'Shut your mouth. Or a sandfly will wander in! Who else but Adam.'

God took the lifeless body of the man He had created and blew His breath into it. And since God created Adam, he had some of God's qualities. When God had blown His being into Adam, He'd filled him with love, mercy, free will . . . and Adam, made of sounding clay, had trembled. Then Adam burst into life with a sneeze!

He spoke his first words. Words that were both a greeting and a prayer. 'All praise and thanks are due to God.'

God then asked His angels to prostrate themselves before Adam as a sign of respect and honour.

Now, there was one angel who had opposed the idea of creating Adam more than the other angels had—with vehemence and bitterness, right from the beginning—when God had sent the angels to bring soil from different corners of the earth. This angel was a djinn.

God had created djinns from fire. They were not angels, nor were they men. But they had the power of reason by which they could distinguish between good and evil. Iblis—that was the name of the protesting djinn—had been so devout in his worship and so faithful in his service to God, that he had become one of the angels.

Iblis was most unhappy at being asked to prostrate himself before Adam. After all, in the order of creation, he came before Adam! So he let his displeasure show, in the way his eyes narrowed and in the way his mouth was set and by continuing to stand his ground.

God turned to Iblis and asked, 'What is your reason for not joining the other angels?'

Now Iblis let his displeasure show in his voice and his words. 'I am not one to prostrate myself before a human being created from sounding clay of altered, smooth mud!'

God was angry. He glowered at Iblis. 'Then get out of here for you have made yourself an outcast, a cursed one. And so you shall remain till the Day of Resurrection.'

So Iblis, the fallen angel, was cast out of God's kingdom and, despite his wrath—in the blackness of his soul—perhaps he was also ashamed of what he had done. Angry with himself, as much as he was with God, he swore to lead Adam astray.

'And so you see, that's why when someone is wicked, they are called Iblis,' Muezza concluded. 'But I meant it in a nice way!' he added hastily, seeing Baby Jaan's eyes well up.

'I know,' she said even as a fat tear rolled down her cheek.

'But Muezza,' she said softly after a while, 'I'm not really Adam's cousin then. I'm Iblis's cousin. I'm a djinn after all.'

'Stop it!' Muezza pulled himself up to his full height. 'We are all God's creatures. Djinn or angel. Cat or camel. Adam or Hawwa,' Muezza thundered. 'Do you hear me?'

Baby Jaan shook her head, trying to shake out the high notes of Muezza's angry voice. *Ouch!* It felt like someone had dropped hot oil into her ears.

'What?' Muezza was watching her.

'I hear you! I hear you! Now calm down!'

Muezza settled back down into a ball. 'You know, Baby Jaan, you shouldn't take every story so personally. These stories are to help us understand how to be better beings, not to beat ourselves up over. God gave us free will. What use is it if we don't exercise it?'

Baby Jaan stared at Muezza. What was the cat talking about? 'Wait a minute,' she said slowly. 'Who is this Hawwa? Angel, djinn or what?'

Muezza groaned.

7

Suddenly Muezza saw a speck on the horizon. It was in the north, which Muezza knew how to identify. One of Shahir's followers liked to gaze at the stars. And on some nights, Muezza watched him watching the stars.

One night he'd pointed to the sky and told his little son, 'Let me teach you how to find your way no matter where you are in the desert. See that . . .' he'd said, pointing to a star, bright and steadfast, in the north, 'stand facing the Pole Star and your left hand will be to the west—that is the direction in which we must bow as we say our prayers.'

'What's there, Abba?' the boy had asked.

'Mecca and the Kaaba.'

'Does the star have a name?' the boy had asked.

'It's called al-Kibblah,' the man had said, and Muezza had memorized the name. That was the north, Muezza had understood then. The sun rose in the east and set in the west. And the one direction left was the south.

And Shahir and his followers had headed south. That much he knew. So it couldn't be them.

'Baby Jaan,' Muezza said, 'someone's coming.'

She looked at him curiously. Muezza sounded worried. 'What's wrong?' she asked, yawning.

'Nothing is wrong . . . but I suggest that you shift your shape to something else!'

Baby Jaan peered at Muezza. 'Why?'

'Won't you do anything till I tell you why?' He sighed. Who knew camels could be such obstinate creatures?

'No . . . no . . . no . . . no . . . no,' Baby Jaan sang.

Muezza flinched. Baby Jaan's voice sounded like mice scampering through his head. He wanted to pounce on it with one swift swipe of his paw.

'We don't know who is coming this way. But whoever it is, if they see you as you are—a white baby camel—they will put a harness around you and take you away,' Muezza explained. 'It's not every day that a white camel appears, and you will be seen as a treasured catch . . .'

'Oh,' Baby Jaan said, her mouth falling open. 'So what shall I become?' she asked.

'How about a camel spider?' Muezza said, cocking an eyebrow. 'Since you are a camel already!' Muezza laughed delicately. He rather liked it when he could crack a joke. Except that his jokes were wasted on a young person like Baby Jaan, which he realized upon seeing her vacant gaze. 'What?' he asked.

'But I don't know what a camel spider looks like . . .' she said, her lower lip wobbling.

'Don't start crying, Baby Jaan!' Muezza said, feeling shame scald him like hot water. It wasn't right to mock a person's ignorance. 'It doesn't matter. And maybe it's best you don't turn into a camel spider. What if they kill you? Tell you what . . . turn into a stone and lie here at the foot of this date palm. I shall climb up and hide there.'

'You're afraid, too.' Baby Jaan giggled.

'It's called being cautious,' Muezza snapped as he curled up into a ball and hid under the crown of leaves. Baby Jaan turned into a rock and stayed half-buried in the sand. No one would give it a second glance.

The speck drew closer and, as Muezza had sensed, it wasn't a trading caravan but a bunch of itinerant nomads. Their faces were covered except for their eyes, and in them Muezza saw a fierceness that made him glad that he was hidden.

'What kind of an oasis is this?' one of them growled, unwinding the keffiyeh cloth from around his face and revealing a full beard.

'Just an oasis,' the second one retorted.

'What I meant was that this one is like the meat of a scrawny camel high up on a rock-strewn mountain. Too much effort for too little!' the bearded man snapped. 'Besides, it was just a rhetorical question.'

His brothers were stupider than stupid, he often thought when he looked at the three of them. He was the leader of the group, and then there were his brothers—the fat one, the short one and the young one. All of them had set out on a raiding mission. He walked away and led his camel to the pond. The others did as he did.

They let the camels drink and then the men gathered under the tree Muezza was crouching in. Soon one of them handed out food for all to eat.

'I need something to rest my head on,' said the young one.

'The young master is missing his silk bolster!' the short brother mocked him.

'I don't know about you lot, but I worry that a cockroach will creep into my ears,' the young man explained.

'A cockroach in a desert!' The three laughed as if he had cracked a joke. 'What about a crocodile?' the fat brother sneered.

'I don't care what you think but I won't put my head on the sand!' the young man retorted.

'I told you, bringing him on this raid was a bad idea,' the fat brother jeered.

'He has to learn our ways one day or the other. Here,' the bearded man said, nudging out the rock with his foot, 'use this as your headrest.'

The young man wrapped his keffiyeh around his eyes and ears, and lay on the sand with his head resting on the rock that was Baby Jaan.

Muezza held her breath. There was no knowing with Baby Jaan. What she would do next was anyone's guess.

The fat brother and the short brother laughed and slapped each other's backs. But soon a fight broke out between the two men. The bearded brother glared at them.

'Enough,' he growled. 'Get back on your mounts. We leave right now!' Then he prodded the sleeping man with his foot. 'Get up,' he roared. 'We are leaving.'

The young man glared back at him.

'What?' the leader hissed.

'Nothing,' said the young man. He stood up, then reached down for the rock and raised it above his head.

The men stared. *What was he going to do?* The leader of the group reached for the dagger in his belt. But the young man simply walked to the pool and threw the rock in, which sank with a loud splash.

'Let's go,' he mumbled.

Nobody said anything for a moment, till the fat one asked, 'What did you do that for?'

'If I hadn't, I would have smashed it on one of your heads!' the young man explained. 'You disturbed my rest, and I don't like to be disturbed. And since you understand only the language of violence, I would have to hurt you for it to penetrate your thick skulls!'

The bearded brother smiled secretly as they rode away in the desert. They'd had the young one pegged as a sissy, but it seemed now that he had the makings of a warrior. As for the other two, they were bullies and it was good for them to know this, as well as the other important truth—those who live by the sword, die by it too.

Muezza climbed down the tree and gazed at the pool. How was he going to rescue Baby Jaan? The thought of getting into the pool made his teeth ache.

But he dipped a paw in the water. And just then, a frog jumped out! Muezza looked at the frog longingly, a paw raised to grab it.

'Stop,' the frog croaked as it leapt into the air. What landed on its feet was Baby Jaan!

'Wow, you're a class act!' Muezza said, unable to keep the admiration out of his voice.

Baby Jaan grinned. 'That *was* kinda cool, right?'

Muezza smiled. 'Oh, that it certainly was!'

'Whew . . . I thought you would forget me if I stayed at the bottom of the pool. Though it *is* rather pleasant down there,' Baby Jaan said, shaking herself. Then she looked at Muezza and asked, 'But what were you doing getting into the pool?'

'I was coming in to rescue you, of course,' Muezza said.

'*You were?*' exclaimed Baby Jaan, rubbing her snout against Muezza's back. 'I didn't know cats could swim!'

Muezza shrugged. 'Cats know how to swim. They just don't like to.'

'*And yet you would have?*' Baby Jaan's voice dropped to a whisper.

Muezza didn't respond. It wasn't in his nature to make a song and dance about what others meant to him. He was just a cat. He did what was right without making a fuss about things.

'May I ask you something?' Baby Jaan said.

'What?'

'Who is Hawwa?' She grinned. 'You were going to tell me the story when we got interrupted . . .'

8

God presided over the heavens and all was right in Adam's world. He slept without stirring even once. That is how it is when you know someone is watching over you to ensure you are safe.

When Adam opened his eyes, he saw a beautiful person peering down at him. He sat up in surprise.

'I have never seen you before . . .' he said, wondering if this was an angel or a djinn or some other being he had no name for.

The person smiled at him.

'Do I know you?' Adam persisted. The heavens looked more splendid than ever and Adam was filled with a curious sensation. A quickening of his heart even as he gazed at the person, a tenderness that made him want to caress the person's cheek as though they were a flower that would be bruised by mere touch.

'Not yet.'

'Who sent you here?' Adam asked, now more curious than ever.

'God sent me,' the person said. The voice reminded him of birdsong.

'Oh,' Adam said, standing up. The person rose to stand alongside him.

'Adam, God knows that in time, you will grow lonely.'

'Lonely? Why would I be?' Adam laughed. The angels were with him all the time.

'The angels have things to do for God and when they go, you will be alone,' the person's voice was soft but firm.

'And . . .?' Adam asked, looking away. The very thought of being all by himself was unsettling.

'And therefore God made me, so I could be with you; as you will be with me. So neither of us is lonely, and both will bring tranquillity into each other's lives.'

Adam held out his hand. The person took it. They smiled at each other and then, with shining eyes, they asked of each other, 'Did you feel it?'

'Yes,' they replied together.

'A singing of the soul, a flowering within . . .'

'What do you think it is?' the person asked.

'A certainty that you will be there for me, as I will be there for you. And that I am you and you are me,' Adam said.

God in His heaven smiled. Adam had his companion.

That's when the angels came and, seeing a person standing with Adam, they asked him, 'Who is this?'

Adam had an answer now. 'This is Hawwa.' He explained, 'It means the living. She is a part of me and I am a living being. So that is her name.'

Adam looked at Hawwa again. He suddenly felt stronger with her by his side.

Baby Jaan's eyes were wide with wonder. 'So this Hawwa is the first woman like Adam was the first man?' she demanded of Muezza.

'Our girl is getting smarter by the moment,' Muezza said, cocking an eyebrow.

'You think so?' Baby Jaan asked, trying to raise an eyebrow like Muezza.

'What are you doing?' Muezza yelled, horrified by Baby Jaan's contorted face.

'I was trying to raise an eyebrow!' Baby Jaan said.

'Don't . . . you're terrifying me.'

'But I want to learn to raise my eyebrows like you . . .' she declared, stomping on the ground.

'For that, my girl, you need to practise. And not throw a tantrum,' Muezza said, yawning loudly.

Baby Jaan's mouth tightened. That sounded precisely like what Umm Jaan said to her. And where *were* her parents? Shouldn't they be looking for her?

'Don't go to sleep. I have something to ask you,' she said suddenly.

Muezza tucked his head into his chest. 'What now? A cat needs his sleep, you know . . .'

'A girl needs her answers, you know . . .' Baby Jaan retorted.

'Can't it wait?' Muezza asked. 'I really, really need a catnap . . .'

And he closed his eyes even though he knew Baby Jaan hadn't even asked him her question yet.

When Muezza awoke, he saw a pair of large, disembodied eyes peering at him. He leapt in the air, frightened out of his wits.

The pair of eyes shifted shape to become Baby Jaan.

'What were you doing?' he asked.

'I was looking over you,' Baby Jaan said.

'Well, you could do that without turning into a pair of eyes without a face!' Muezza shuddered.

'I guess, but I was practising like you asked me to,' she said, turning into a pair of eyes again—one that could cock an eyebrow. 'And it's easier to do it when I'm just a pair of eyes rather than a whole face!' Her voice came out of nowhere.

Muezza stiffened. Cats preyed on anything that looked remotely pouncable or catchable. He couldn't help himself; a cat had to do what a cat had to do.

The pair of eyes hastily turned back into Baby Jaan, complete with an idiotic grin.

Muezza was relieved. 'Didn't you want to ask me something?'

The sun was dipping towards the horizon and Baby Jaan yawned.

'This Hawwa,' she said after she'd completed three yawns in quick succession, 'where did she come from?'

Muezza smiled. 'God made her.'

'Yes, I know. But what did he make her out of? He made Adam out of clay; and of what was left he made a camel. So what remained to make Hawwa from?' Baby Jaan's mouth stretched into a crafty smile.

Muezza laid his head on his paws. *Darn!* He had forgotten. Where on earth *did* this Hawwa come from? Then he remembered.

One evening, Shahir was getting ready to leave when he heard loud voices and wailing from one of the outer rooms. So Shahir rushed out to find the reason for the commotion. And he saw that one of his distant cousins had a slave woman tied up and was beating her with a coil of rope.

'Stop!' Shahir thundered. 'What do you think you are doing?'

'She . . . th-this slave . . .' the cousin said, his face red with rage, 'will not marry me. As my wife, she will have the best of everything. But she doesn't want to!'

'And you are beating her into submission?' Shahir asked in a dangerously soft voice.

'Yes,' the man said. 'That's what you do to any creature that won't listen. Tame them into submission!'

'Do you know who women have descended from?' Shahir asked.

'Hawwa . . .' The man shrugged.

'Do you know that God made Hawwa from Adam's rib? The upper part of the rib is crooked. If you try to straighten it, the rib will break. If you leave it, the rib will stay crooked forever,' Shahir said.

'What do you suggest I do?' The cousin fell at Shahir's feet. His rage was replaced by distress. He didn't know what to do. He had fallen in love with the girl but she seemed to hate the sight of him.

'Be gentle with her. Treat her with kindness. Remember, she is a part of you. When you hurt her, you hurt yourself. And when she sees the kindness in you, she will start seeing you as a man worthy of her love. Ask her then to be your wife,' Shahir said, walking away.

Muezza, who had followed Shahir, had heard it all.

It was this that he narrated to Baby Jaan; and as he came to the end of the story, he saw that her eyelids were drooping.

'Go to sleep, Baby Jaan,' he said gently. She was a child after all.

She sighed and put her head down. And then snuggled up to Muezza.

Soon stars appeared in the skies. Muezza stared at them and wondered where his Shahir was. It was already his second night in the desert with Baby Jaan.

9

Muezza felt a small curl of sadness unfurl within him. Had his Shahir forgotten him?

No, it wasn't possible! Shahir *would* come seeking him.

He thought of the time he had fallen asleep on Shahir's robe one winter evening. It had been a cold day and as the sun fell, Muezza had felt freezing fingers run down his spine.

His usual sunny spot on the floor had been as cold as a block of ice, and his other favourite spot—the golden-yellow cushion—was being used by a visitor as a backrest. But Muezza had seen a perfect place to curl up on. It was soft and fleecy, and lay in a corner far away from scampering children and chattering adults. Muezza had leapt on to it and gone to sleep.

When Muezza had woken up, there was a group of people gathered around Shahir, exclaiming at his coat that seemed to be missing one sleeve. 'Whatever happened?' they were saying.

'Muezza was asleep on my robe. I didn't want to disturb him. So I cut the coat sleeve off the robe. Fortunately I didn't wake him.' Shahir smiled.

'You ruined your robe for a cat?' someone exclaimed in disbelief.

'For my Muezza, I will do anything,' Shahir said. 'Like I would do for you. He is as much God's child as you and I are.'

Muezza had felt a lump in his throat.

He'd got up and gone towards Shahir. Then he'd prostrated himself before Shahir to show his love, respect and gratitude. Shahir had reached down and stroked his head.

Muezza could feel the imprint of his fingers even now. For as long as he would live, he would feel the kindliness of his Shahir's touch. Would such a Shahir abandon him?

No. Muezza shook his head and curled up against Baby Jaan.

Muezza woke up with a start, as if someone had just thrown a heavy wooden chest down a staircase. He sat up and looked around him. Then he heard it again. This was a sound that had no business being here at this time of the year. And again the sound tore through the skies.

Thunder.

He stretched and looked up. And there it was—a rumble that grew in the horizon and then, with a speed that startled even Muezza, it crashed right above Baby Jaan and him.

Baby Jaan leapt in the air so high that Muezza thought she would disappear among the clouds! Then she landed beside him with a soft thud.

'What on earth was that?' And looking at the open-mouthed Muezza, she demanded, 'And what's with you?'

'You were levitating!' Muezza said in an almost accusatory tone.

'No, I wasn't. I'm not *that* sort of person,' she said angrily. 'I am a well-brought-up Jaan!'

'Baby Jaan, do you know what levitating means?' Muezza laughed.

Baby Jaan blinked. Then shook her head. 'Doesn't it mean I brought up the contents of my intestines?'

'That's regurgitating! To levitate is to rise above the ground.'

'Oh!' Baby Jaan grinned. She shook her head again. 'Got mixed up, I guess.'

'But Baby Jaan, I'm very, very impressed. You know what regurgitate means!' Muezza said.

'Abby Jaan likes to use big words,' she said and then peered at him. 'Aren't we forgetting something?'

'What?'

Just then the skies rumbled again.

'That!' she said, rolling her eyes. '*What is that?*'

'That is thunder,' he said as the night sky dazzled with a jagged burst of light. 'And *that* is lightning.'

Baby Jaan flinched and leaned towards Muezza. 'I'm scared,' she said in a small voice.

'Nothing to be scared of.' Muezza smiled as the skies continued to rumble and grumble with flashes of lightning lighting up the desert.

'What's going to happen?' Baby Jaan whispered.

Then a drop fell. A gentle *plop* on Baby Jaan's snout and a little *tap* on Muezza's head.

'Wow!' Baby Jaan cried.

'*Eww . . .*' Muezza shrieked. 'Rain—that's what's going to happen!'

Baby Jaan closed her eyes. This rain thing felt good. 'Isn't it lovely?' she said. Baby Jaan felt her heart sing and her legs twitch, ready to dance.

'Are you out of your mind?' Muezza hissed. 'I hate getting wet!'

'Hmm . . . in that case—' said Baby Jaan, and became a beautiful white parasol to protect Muezza.

'Very nice!' Muezza said, who by now had ceased to be amazed at Baby Jaan's shape-shifting. 'But you realize that you're letting the rain through, right? You need to be waterproof!'

The parasol jumped up and down. 'What's waterproof?' it demanded.

'Never mind . . .' Muezza sighed.

Suddenly the water stopped passing through. Muezza snuggled under the parasol that was successfully keeping him bone dry.

'I think we have what you call a win-win situation,' the parasol-turned-umbrella chortled.

'Meaning?'

'Meaning you're dry and I'm wet. You stay out of the rain and I get to enjoy the rain!' the umbrella said in such a cheery voice that Muezza felt like kicking it. How could anybody enjoy the rain?

'Baby Jaan,' Muezza said thoughtfully as the rain fell, 'I think you very well may be the desert's first waterproof umbrella. Speaking of which, how did you know about the parasol?'

'I saw a woman hold one above another woman in a caravan . . .' Baby Jaan said.

At first Baby Jaan hadn't known what was going on. Why was one woman holding a strange thing above another's head while her own head was unprotected? That's when Baby Jaan had seen a familiar shape land a little ahead of her. Purple-haired with blue eyebrows and a nose that was scimitar-sharp if she was furious or peach-soft if she was smiling. The tail—

that turned into a bushy stole if she was cold or into a fan if she was warm—was wrapped around her head like a turban to protect her from the desert sun. Jiddat Eazima Jaan. Baby Jaan's great-grandmother had arrived with a group of lady Jaans who always seemed to shadow her.

Jiddat Eazima had frowned at the sight of Baby Jaan on her own. Her nose had already begun turning into a scimitar when it stopped and retreated to being round and fuzzy. She forgot to be angry, struck as Baby Jaan had been by the parasol.

'I want one of those,' she'd said firmly to the lady Jaans, clicking her fingers.

One of the ladies had turned into a parasol and Baby Jaan had seen how it was done! The trick was to hold yourself in the shape of the thing you wanted to become. But of course, like any skill, it required practise.

Jiddat Eazima had gone on her way, shielded by a parasol, while another lady Jaan had held it over her head. But before Jiddat Eazima had left, she'd sent off a servant Jaan to become a gust of wind to toss the parasol from the woman's hand and send it far, far away. Jiddat Eazima was like that. She didn't like others having what she did.

The rain continued to fall and Muezza could see a puddle grow near them. Soon the umbrella wouldn't suffice, he realized. But he didn't know what Baby Jaan could do to help.

'Baby Jaan,' he said suddenly. 'Looks like I'm going to be cast out of this warm space. Like Adam and Hawwa were . . .'

The umbrella stood upright for a moment. 'Is there a story there?'

'Why?' Muezza asked.

And before Muezza could say 'God help us', Baby Jaan became a beautiful white tent, complete with a ground sheet and a soft, white cushion!

'Tell me the story,' Baby Jaan demanded.

Grandly, Muezza curled up on the cushion and wrapped his tail around his neck. He thought he was beginning to get a sore throat.

'Remember your cousins, Adam and Hawwa?'

Adam and Hawwa were as happy in jannat as happy could be. God told them to eat freely with pleasure all that there was, and to delight in things wherever they found anything to delight them. But He did warn them to not go near a particular tree. It will turn you into wrongdoers, He'd said.

Adam and Hawwa did as God asked them to. God watched them as He watched over the universe. God, the benevolent one, had given them the best of His gifts: free will. The freedom to choose. But free will comes with great responsibility. That of using it carefully. For free will also comes with consequences.

All this while, Iblis had been waiting. The thing about anger, revenge and evil is that it becomes viler as it waits. Iblis had been cast out of paradise but he knew how to creep into the thoughts of Adam and Hawwa. All it took was to be a whisper in the ear, an ache in the foot, an eyelash in the eye.

Iblis understood Adam and Hawwa. He knew how to reach them from their front and back, their right and left. He knew how to play on the weak spots in Adam's and Hawwa's minds. And so he whispered to them again and again about that particular tree in jannat.

God had never said that Adam or Hawwa *couldn't* eat its fruit. God hadn't forbidden them anything. But Iblis knew exactly what to tell them.

'Maybe the tree has powers. Maybe it's because God doesn't want you to become angels or know something that only God knows. Who knows indeed! Why didn't God warn the angels then?' he murmured.

Soon Adam and Hawwa could think of nothing else except the fruit of that particular tree. And one day, unable to bear it any longer, Adam and Hawwa plucked a low-hanging fruit.

As soon as they ate it and then looked at each other, they knew shame. That they were naked, they realized. They grabbed leaves and began covering themselves up. And then they waited for God's anger.

But God forgave them as God always does. God had known it was going to happen. And He knew that this would prepare Adam and Hawwa to be caretakers of the earth.

Adam and Hawwa had learnt first-hand how crafty Iblis was and how he could misguide and deceive them. God also wanted them to know that their expulsion from heaven was only a short punishment and when they had lived on earth for a while, they could return to jannat if they were not led astray by Iblis again.

So Adam, Hawwa and their descendants would dwell on earth. That was God's decree. And on a Friday, Adam and Hawwa descended to earth.

It is said that the best of days on which the sun has risen is Friday. And it was on this day that Adam was created, and on this day that he descended to earth.

'That was how Adam and Hawwa came to live on earth,' Muezza finished.

There was no response from Baby Jaan.

'Are you all right?' he asked.

The tent shook vigorously. 'No,' she said, 'I am not all right.'

10

Muezza lay on his back, stretching out his paws beneath his head. 'Stop shaking, Baby Jaan,' he said. 'You're making me nervous. What if you collapse on me?'

The tent strained on its pegs in indignation. 'I don't know if anyone has told you this but you are one selfish cat. Do you think of anyone but yourself?'

Muezza took a deep breath. How was he to explain to Baby Jaan that fish swam, birds flew and cats were self-centred? If only she knew what an effort he was making to be considerate.

'What did I do now?' he asked, sighing.

'I told you I was not all right. And you didn't ask why!' Baby Jaan sounded like she was almost in tears.

'What's wrong?' he asked, nuzzling his head against the tent.

'Do you realize that Iblis is a djinn and so am I? What if I become another Iblis?'

Muezza nuzzled his head against the tent some more. 'Iblis is Iblis and you are Baby Jaan, the sweetest baby djinn in the world. It doesn't matter who we are born as; we can *choose* to be good or evil.'

Baby Jaan sighed. 'That's easy for you to say.'

Muezza stretched and sat back on the cushion. 'Looks like it will rain a little longer and so I'm going to tell you one more story. This is the story of the first crime on earth. And you will understand why I said that it is up to you to choose who you want to be. Remember, Baby Jaan, God gave us free will.'

Baby Jaan groaned. Why did Muezza sound like a schoolmaster at times? All big words and 'he-said-and-she-said' . . .

Baby Jaan had been told about the djinn school that she was supposed to attend every full-moon day. And she had sneaked a peek at one run by an elderly Jaan who'd become blackboard and chalk, cane and wastepaper basket. As for the djinn students, they'd turn into desk, book and pen, and sometimes motes of dust that the djinn schoolmaster swatted by turning into a feather duster. Baby Jaan had decided to stay away from school if she could. And here was Muezza being a schoolmaster—treating her like an idiot just because she didn't know words that had more than two syllables.

Baby Jaan rolled her eyes and looked at the sky. That's when she realized that it had stopped raining. But Muezza hadn't realized that! And she wasn't going to tell him till he finished the story.

Adam and Hawwa left jannat, and began their life on earth. God had prepared them for this new life, right from teaching them the names of everything living and their usefulness, to giving them first-hand experience of how cunning Iblis and his whispers could be.

Adam was the first prophet of God on earth. It was his duty to establish the laws of God here, and to fill the earth with people who would live by God's word, care for and improve the earth. Adam knew earth couldn't ever become jannat but he could try to make it similar to paradise.

Soon Adam and Hawwa had two sons, Qabil and Habil. Qabil was the older son and he ploughed the land. Habil was the younger son and the one who raised livestock. All was well until it was time for them to marry. Qabil was not happy with his bride. He preferred the one chosen for Habil.

But was it then that trouble began? Or had Iblis already lain seeds of hate by whispering in Qabil's ears, asking him questions that he had never thought of until then . . .

Do you think your father, Adam, prefers your brother to you? Why is it that your mother, Hawwa, gives Habil the larger share of the dates? Didn't the two of you work equally hard all day? Why is it that your father always has a joke for Habil and your mother can never stop caressing his cheek? But when it comes to you, all they have is a list of chores for you to do? So who are you? Are you not their son?

Qabil tried to ignore the insinuations but eventually Iblis's whispers wore him out. His hatred for Habil began to grow by the day.

Envy, that onyx-eyed imp, came to live in Qabil's eyes and thoughts. Everything Habil had, Qabil envied him for. Why did Habil get to tend to animals, which was an easier job, while he had to toil in the sun and rain, breaking the soil, planting crops and harvesting them?

One day, when God decreed that the two brothers make a sacrifice, Qabil offered his worst grain to God and Habil offered his best animals—healthy, fat and handsome.

God looked at the two. If Qabil had offered the broken and rotten grain because he'd had nothing else, God would have accepted it with love and joy. But God knew that Qabil had large reserves of plump, full-bodied grain. And so God turned away from Qabil's offering and accepted Habil's animals.

Qabil was angrier than ever. But he kept his anger to himself, till one day when Habil didn't return by dusk. When Qabil reached home, he saw his father pacing outside and his mother wringing her hands and sobbing.

'What's wrong?' Qabil asked Adam.

'It's way past sunset and your brother isn't home yet!' Adam said, holding his palm over his eyes and peering at the horizon.

'I'm quite certain something has happened to him,' Hawwa said, coming towards them.

Qabil felt that lump of rage in him become denser, tighter. He had reached home late, too, but neither of his parents seemed perturbed by it. He would have been happy if they had tossed even a cursory crumb his way—'Qabil, what happened? Why were you late?'

Instead Adam said, 'Qabil, go look for your brother. We cannot rest in peace till you bring him home.'

Qabil was hot and tired, sweaty and hungry; but he had to leave. And all Qabil could feel was a blackness descending on him. He grabbed the iron rod he used for digging holes in the ground and set off. Who knew what dangers he would have to encounter in the dark? When he would see Habil, he would give him a good beating first, he decided as he trudged wearily.

Soon Qabil found Habil in a quiet place away from the sight of Adam and Hawwa. And his anger towards Habil flared up again. 'The favourite son, always the favourite son—what about me? Am I not their child?' he asked himself. 'I saved the best of the grain for them so that they don't go hungry. But do they realize that, or does their God? Instead all they see is that God didn't accept my sacrifice, and so I'm the bad one!'

'Hello, brother,' Habil said as Qabil approached him. 'I was just on my way home.'

Qabil saw the happy smile on Habil's face. But to him it seemed smug, like a crocodile that had swallowed the monkey.

'You look very pleased with yourself,' he said quietly.

'Oh, I am, brother,' Habil said. 'What's not to be pleased about?'

'In that case, what if I told you that your time on earth is coming to an end?'

'What do you mean?' Habil asked, taking a step backwards.

There was an ominous quiet as the night swirled around them. Dense blackness was creeping in and leeching away the light.

'I am going to kill you!' he told Habil.

The younger one saw a murderous glint in his older brother's eyes. He was scared but he wanted to make peace. So he said, 'Brother, you can do what you choose, kill me even. But I won't raise my hand against you for I fear God . . .'

Qabil sank his iron rod deep into the soil. 'And who is this God?'

'The lord of mankind, djinns and all that exists,' Habil said, turning to go.

Qabil could bear it no longer. He raised the rod and brought it down on Habil's head.

The tent disappeared and Muezza found himself on a sand dune, which, mercifully, was dry. Baby Jaan sat crouched near Muezza. There were tears rolling down her camel cheeks.

'And so, Habil—what happened to him? Do tell me nothing happened to him!'

Muezza shook his head. 'Baby Jaan, he died.'

'*Died?* What's died?' she asked in a curious voice. She had never heard the word before.

'Hmm . . .' Muezza said, searching for an answer. 'He didn't talk; he didn't walk; he didn't know hunger or thirst; he couldn't laugh or cry. He stopped breathing. Baby Jaan . . . that is death. A sleep you don't wake up from.'

Baby Jaan stared at Muezza.

Death. Djinns didn't die. Or she hadn't heard of djinns dying. But man did. She knew that now.

'And then what happened?' she asked. 'Was Qabil happy that he no longer had Habil to make him angry or jealous?'

Muezza shook his head and pondered. Life was never that simple, and Qabil's story was both a lesson and a tragedy.

'I need to rest, Baby Jaan,' he said. 'I'm tired and my mind isn't working any more.'

Muezza closed his eyes. The truth was Muezza didn't have the stomach to finish the story at that point. Human fallibility made him weary.

11

Baby Jaan stayed awake. She didn't know if djinns slept. Ever since she had met Muezza, she had taken to grabbing a camel-nap—she refused to call it a catnap. But the thing was, she didn't know if camels napped either. Still, she had learnt to close her eyes and let her mind hop on to a magic carpet.

'Where are Umm Jaan and Abby Jaan?' she wondered aloud. The truth was, she did feel a little abandoned. 'Shouldn't they be looking for me? Like Adam and Hawwa were looking for Habil?' That's when it occurred to her that Muezza hadn't completed the story.

I am slow, she thought, grimacing. Any intelligent djinn would have realized that a long time ago but, me being me, I thought the story had ended with Qabil hitting Habil on his head!

'Muezza, get up.' Baby Jaan prodded him in his side.

'Ouch!' Muezza shrieked, hissing and spitting. 'Don't ever do that!'

'Whoa!' Baby Jaan said, surprised by the vehemence of Muezza's reaction. 'What did you get so scared for?'

'At my last count, I was into my fourth life . . . and I don't want to squander what's left of it,' Muezza said, grooming himself so that Baby Jaan wouldn't see how perturbed he was.

'Lives?' Baby Jaan prodded Muezza gently. 'Tell me, Muezza . . . what do you mean?'

'Well, all living creatures live and die . . . That's the nature of life,' Muezza explained.

'Even Adam and Hawwa?' Baby Jaan asked incredulously. She had thought that they would live forever! They were God's children after all.

'Even Adam and Hawwa; in fact, Adam's lifespan was meant to be a thousand years . . .' Muezza said, stretching.

Suddenly Baby Jaan sat up straight. She could hear a whispering wind. 'Muezza,' she said urgently, 'listen to me, a band of Jaans is out looking for me . . .'

Muezza frowned. 'Why aren't you looking happy? Weren't you moaning, just a little while ago, that you felt abandoned . . . because your parents hadn't come looking for you like Adam and Hawwa went looking for Habil?'

'You heard me?' Baby Jaan blushed.

'Catnaps mean catnaps . . . not cat-sleep. You silly child! But shouldn't you signal them that you are here?'

'Then they will find me. And I don't want to go,' Baby Jaan said, planting her feet firmly in the sand.

'But why?'

'I can't leave you on your own, Muezza. You are my friend. And my me-n-t-or, too,' Baby Jaan groped for the words. 'The desert is no place for a cat. Till your Shahir comes to fetch you, I will be a burr on your fur!' she added with a grin.

Muezza would have hugged Baby Jaan if he knew how to. But cats didn't hug. They were not into public displays of affection either. So he twitched his whiskers and said, 'Fair enough!'

Fair enough, indeed, Baby Jaan thought. Couldn't Muezza just give her a hug? Did he even realize what she was doing for him?

Muezza touched Baby Jaan with his paw. 'I don't do hugs, Baby Jaan. And I don't do licking of the face or wagging of my tail.'

'Fair enough,' Baby Jaan retorted, wondering if Muezza knew how to read minds.

Muezza grinned at her feistiness. The wind was no longer whispering. 'What are we going to do when your army of Jaans gets here? Where will you hide?'

'I have an idea,' Baby Jaan said, turning into a scarab.

'Change back!' Muezza hissed. 'Are you out of your mind?'

Baby Jaan turned back into her white camel self. She scowled. 'Can't you hold yourself back for once? You don't have to swat every beetle you see . . .'

Muezza glared at her. He felt his tail stiffening in anger. 'You idiot,' he said. 'That's exactly why! What cat, unless it is a nincompoop, would sit clutching a scarab to its bosom? The Jaans would be instantly suspicious!'

Baby Jaan's jaw fell open. 'Wow! You *are* smart. Must be all the fish you eat . . . brain food!'

'Stop talking and think of what you can be . . .' Muezza said, pretending not to be pleased.

'I did mean it, you know,' Baby Jaan said, turning into a burr that then clung to Muezza's fur.

Just in time, Muezza thought, as the swooshing wind turned into an army of cats! The chief cat must be the general leading the troops, Muezza presumed. Who on earth was Baby Jaan, he wondered, for an entire army to be out looking for her . . .

'Greetings, brother,' the cat general said in a deep mew.

Muezza's thoughts jumped to one of the generals who had come to meet Shahir. Did all generals have a deep voice and a formal tone? Did they become generals because they had a deep voice and used a formal tone? Or did being a general give them a voice that sounded like a cane being struck against the bottom of a barrel and manners that made them say 'Hello, how do you do?' to a mosquito before slapping it dead?

'*Greetings, brother!*' the general said again, rather impatiently this time.

'Greetings, brother,' Muezza replied in as deep a mew as he could muster.

'Our princess is missing from the palace,' the general said.

'I didn't know there was a cat kingdom . . .' Muezza said in his most artless voice.

'There isn't. We are Jaans. Shape-shifters. We chose to be cats because you are one.'

'What does your princess look like?' Muezza asked.

The general thought for a moment and looked at his troops. They looked back at him with open mouths. What indeed did she look like? They wondered, too.

The general cleared his throat. 'As we are shape-shifters, she could be anything. But she is a baby. So the chances are she may either appear as a beetle or a ball, a crab or a caterpillar, an egg or a jug . . . I don't think she would know how to transform herself into anything else . . .'

'Is that so?' Muezza said, stifling a laugh. 'So if I spot a beetle or a ball, a crab or a caterpillar, an egg or a jug, I shall certainly keep an eye out for it.'

'Do that, and if you let us know, there will be a reward. Anything you want!' the cat general said. 'Here,' he said, offering a whistle on a string. 'Blow it and we will find you no matter where you are.'

'Is it a magic whistle?' Muezza asked curiously.

The general strung the whistle around Muezza's neck. 'It's a djinn whistle. All you need to do is blow it and a Jaan will find you.'

Muezza nodded and watched in amusement as the cat general clicked his heels and turned. 'Squad! Mark time . . . forward march!' he said and strode ahead. The army followed him. In a few minutes they had turned into a sandstorm that disappeared into the horizon.

'Right, you can show yourself now,' Muezza said. When the burr was once again Baby Jaan, Muezza continued, 'That was scary. I think I may have used up my fifth life as well.'

'Oh, Jaans are mostly harmless!' Baby Jaan giggled. 'They are not like Palis or Guls. We are a laid-back lot.'

'The general didn't seem laid-back. It seemed like he would've liked to tear me to bits but was just being a gentlemanly soldier and holding himself back.'

'Well, he is all bluster and whiskers but he is really just a pussycat.' Baby Jaan grinned. 'But tell me, what is this thing about fourth and fifth lives? How many do you have?'

Muezza stretched almost as if he were preening, Baby Jaan thought. Then he looked through his eyelashes. 'Nine.'

'*Nine!*' Baby Jaan shrieked and fell on her back.

'Baby Jaan! Baby Jaan!' Muezza exclaimed, leaping to her side.

12

Baby Jaan looked at him with a stupefied expression. 'Why would a cat have nine lives when even Adam has just one?'

Muezza wondered if he should propound his theory but he wasn't sure if even Baby Jaan would believe it. That was the problem with lateral thinking, he thought. Convincing the other was tougher than letting the mind wander on a trajectory of its own.

'Tell me, tell me . . .' Baby Jaan bounced on her feet. 'How can a cat have nine lives?'

Muezza sighed. It was almost dawn and all signs of rain had disappeared. In fact, the happenings of the night seemed more like a dream. Baby Jaan, a princess? Nah! Muezza decided, shaking his head.

'It happened before my time and so it begins with hearsay . . .' Muezza began. 'My Shahir had a favourite companion. His name was Abu Hurayrah. He was one of the important preachers who carried forth the word of God. And he was called Abu Hurayrah because he was really fond of cats and carried a cat in his bag everywhere he went.

'One day, a deadly snake crawled into the sleeve of Shahir's robe, which hung from a peg. Shahir finished his ablutions and prayers, and decided to go out with Abu Hurayrah.

'As Shahir removed the robe from the peg, the cat in Abu Hurayrah's bag leapt out and made a lightning strike on the sleeve of the robe. Everyone stared in surprise, it was as if the cat had lost its mind.

'When the snake slithered out, the cat pounced on it and killed it with one swift move of her paw and jaw. Everyone gasped imagining what could have happened to Shahir. As for Abu Hurayrah, he couldn't stop exclaiming, "All praise is due to God, the Lord of the Universe; the beneficent, the merciful; the Lord of the Day of Judgement. You alone we worship, and you alone we turn to for help!"

'But Shahir just smiled and stroked the cat's head. His fingers left three marks on the cat's forehead, which became part of a cat's markings. And since Shahir had left the impressions of his fingers on the cat, it so happened that cats would never fall on their backs.

'See, cats always land on their feet. And so it helps us get out of situations. Which is why I believe that cats have nine lives!' Muezza ended with a flourish.

He waited for Baby Jaan to argue about the logic of his argument. Mock him even. But all she said was, 'Makes sense, Muezza.'

Then she looked at him through her eyelashes and said, 'But how do you know that this is what happened?'

'Oh, the cat who saved Shahir from the snake was my great-grandmother and she told me the story herself,' Muezza thought of his old *eazima*, who had been a treasure house of stories and sayings.

Baby Jaan shuddered. Her great-grandmother was a 'term-a-gant'—whatever that was. She had heard one of her uncles say that to her father. On a bad day, her great-grandmother would turn into a creature that breathed fire. On a not-so-bad day, she would turn into a pyramid of cups that would smash into smithereens just as someone walked past. Or she would turn into a cobweb that would keep moving no matter how much a house djinn tried to reach it.

Maybe I have never given her a chance, Baby Jaan thought with a pang. Maybe I should crawl into her lap and demand a story!

'Yes, you should do that,' Muezza said softly.

Baby Jaan blinked in shock. So he *did* know how to read minds. But whoever heard of a cat that could read minds?

'I know I should. But Muezza . . .' Her voice dropped. 'She has that old djinn smell!' Baby Jaan wrinkled her nose.

Muezza shrugged. 'When you are a baby, you smell of milk. When you are young, you smell of energy. When you are old, you smell of resignation and quiet. That's nature's way, Baby Jaan. Learn to embrace it.'

Baby Jaan nodded. She would. But maybe first she should ask Umm Jaan to gift her eazima a flagon of attar and the house djinn to light incense in her room.

'Good idea,' Muezza said slyly.

Baby Jaan looked away, too afraid to think. It seemed Muezza could read her every thought just as if she had spoken it aloud.

'And what happened after Qabil hit Habil on his head?' she asked, remembering the unfinished story of the first crime.

Muezza stretched. 'I have a new name for you,' he said with a big grin.

'What,' Baby Jaan asked, 'is my name?'

'PP. Persistent Princess. Or Pest Princess! Don't you ever stop? I have never heard of any creature with such a hunger, apart from the whale that swallowed Prophet Yunus!'

Muezza grinned. He knew Baby Jaan would soon clamour to hear about the whale.

She made a face. Such a horrible face that Muezza almost retched. The last time he'd felt as disgusted was when he had spotted a six-day-dead rat. *Ewwww!*

'Don't . . .' he said in a faint voice.

'Well, if you don't want me to show you my other awful faces, stop calling me silly names and tell me about Qabil and what happened next,' Baby Jaan said in a silky voice.

Muezza rolled his eyes and cleared his throat.

Qabil looked down at his dead brother and didn't know what to do. He didn't dare go back home and face his parents' wrath. But neither did he want to leave his brother lying in the middle of nowhere for him to be pecked at by vultures and crows or torn to bits by hyenas or rats. So he hoisted his brother's corpse over his shoulder. Ploughing the fields had made him broad of shoulder and strong of arm.

For three whole days, it is said, Qabil roamed the earth burdened by his brother's dead body and his own uneasiness that ate at him like ants chewing on a piece of sugar cane—bit by bit, drawing juice and sweetness—till all he knew within was the chalky taste of chewed-up wood. For he didn't even have a name for how he felt.

It was time for God to step in.

On the third evening as Qabil rested by a rock, he saw two crows fly towards him. Soon they started fighting over a scrap of something. The fight became more vicious as the crows began to peck at each other. Finally one crow killed the other. As Qabil watched, the victorious crow dug a hole in the ground with its beak and dragged the vanquished crow into it. After this, it covered the corpse with mud and stones. Then the crow flew away, leaving Qabil with a sense of remorse. For he realized now the enormity of what he had done. He had taken a life.

For how could anyone who cannot give life take it?

And he hadn't even known what the crow knew. That you must honour the dead.

He hung his head in shame and wept. 'I have been wicked and led by Iblis. I forgot the word of God, and look at me—I am the lowest of the low, since for wisdom I need to watch a crow!'

He buried Habil in a hole in the ground and slunk away.

The first crime on earth had been committed and it had resulted from envy. A brother's envy for what his brother had.

13

There was a long silence after Muezza had finished his story of Qabil and Habil and the first crime on earth.

'If I had a brother, I would love him,' Baby Jaan said.

'Would you love a sister as much?' Muezza asked. 'When I was a kitten and till I was a young cat, my siblings and I were inseparable. Not any more. Now we live under the same roof but are not necessarily friends. It has to do with being a cat. Cats are solitary creatures, not like pack animals that need each other to survive.'

'What about my cousin Adam or the other djinns? Do we *need* each other?' Baby Jaan asked. The Jaans were always together.

Muezza shrugged. 'I don't know.'

'But how can you not know? You know everything!' said Baby Jaan, her eyes round with amazement.

'I'm flattered you think so,' Muezza replied with a small smile. 'But I'm just a little cat . . .'

The sun was climbing in the sky, and neither cat nor djinn could live on stories alone. They looked at each other, asking, 'What do we do?'

'What do Jaans eat?' Muezza asked, still hoping that they were vegetarians.

'I'm so hungry that I could eat a tent with an Arab in it!' claimed Baby Jaan.

'You're joking, aren't you?' Muezza asked, taking a little step backwards.

'Am I?' Baby Jaan said, turning into an enormous Venus flytrap. 'All I know now is that I'm a hungry mouth!'

'In that case, let's find you some food,' Muezza said, standing up. 'And can you please become your original self?'

The Venus flytrap turned back into a baby camel. 'We are what we feel,' Baby Jaan said. 'So if I am feeling hungry, you know the rest . . .' she said, trotting at Muezza's side.

The oasis was hardly more than a quick halt-point. Probably a place in which to wait out if a desert storm came, or adjust the stirrups on a horse. It was truly a godforsaken spot and hopefully Iblis-forsaken as well, Muezza thought. There was nothing at all at the oasis.

'What do we do?' they asked each other again.

'I have heard that sometimes Bedouins who have a fixed route bury their supplies. But where on this oasis do we look for it?' Muezza asked, looking at the expanse around them. It really was a tiny oasis . . . till you decided to dig it up.

'But how do we find it?' Baby Jaan asked. 'I could become a spade . . .'

'Yes, but what use is that?' Muezza snorted.

Then he got that glazed look in his eyes that Baby Jaan was beginning to recognize.

'I just had a brainwave!' he exclaimed with great excitement.

'Oh,' Baby Jaan said. She had thought he'd had an idea. But now it seemed like it was something else. 'Are you in pain? Does your head hurt?'

Muezza shook his head. 'What nonsense are you talking about, Baby Jaan? Why would I be in pain?'

'But you said you had a brainwave . . .'

Muezza hit his head with his paw a few times. 'You are such a nincompoop, camel! Brainwave means a brilliant idea . . .'

Baby Jaan grinned. She hadn't been wrong after all. 'So what *was* the brainwave?'

'Well, you could turn into a hound or a rat. Both creatures can sniff out scents very easily . . .' Muezza suggested.

'So do I become a hound? Or a rat?'

Muezza narrowed his eyes. Now that was a toughie!

Once Baby Jaan turned into a hound, what if she decided to tear him apart for sport? If she turned into a rat, all he had to do was rein in his natural impulses. That, he thought, would take effort, but he knew how to hold himself in check. He had learnt from Shahir himself what he should do. The ninety-nine names of God—he just had to recite them and he would know how to hold himself back from attacking Baby Jaan as a rat.

'Rat,' he announced.

Baby Jaan gazed at him for a long moment. Then she looked away for a moment. By the time Muezza blinked, she was a rat—scurrying this way and that, sniffing out the scent of food.

14

Muezza climbed up a date palm, closed his eyes to the sight of a scampering rat and began reciting the ninety-nine names of God.

AL-MALIK · THE ABSOLUTE RULER

AR-RAHIM · THE ALL-MERCIFUL

AR-RAHMAN · THE ALL-COMPASSIONATE

AL-MUHAYMIN · THE GUARDIAN

AL-QUDDUS · THE PURE ONE

AL-AZIZ · THE VICTORIOUS

AL-MU'MIN · THE INSPIRER OF FAITH

AS-SALAM · THE SOURCE OF PEACE

AL-WAHHAB • THE GIVER OF ALL

AL-BARI' • THE MAKER OF ORDER

AL-GHAFFAR • THE FORGIVING

AL-MUSAWWIR • THE SHAPER OF BEAUTY

AL-QAHHAR • THE SUBDUER

AL-KHALIQ • THE CREATOR

Al-Wahhab		The Giver of All
Ar-Razzaq		The Sustainer
Al-Fattah		The Opener
Al-'Alim		The Knower of All
Al-Qabid		The Constrictor
Al-Basit		The Reliever
Al-Khafid		The Abaser
Ar-Rafi		The Exalter
Al-Mu'izz		The Bestower of Honours
Al-Mudhill		The Humiliator
As-Sami		The Hearer of All
Al-Basir		The Seer of All
Al-Hakam		The Judge
Al-'Adl		The Just
Al-Latif		The Subtle One
Al-Khabir		The All-Aware
Al-Halim		The Forbearing
Al-Azim		The Magnificent
Al-Ghafur		The Forgiver and Hider of Faults
Ash-Shakur		The Rewarder of Thankfulness
Al-Ali		The Highest
Al-Kabir		The Greatest
Al-Hafiz		The Preserver
Al-Muqit		The Nourisher
Al-Hasib		The Accounter
Al-Jalil		The Mighty
Al-Karim		The Generous
Ar-Raqib		The Watchful One
Al-Mujib		The Responder to Prayer
Al-Wasi		The All-Comprehending
Al-Hakim		The Perfectly Wise
Al-Wadud		The Loving One
Al-Majid		The Majestic One
Al-Ba'ith		The Resurrector
Ash-Shahid		The Witness
Al-Haqq		The Truth
Al-Wakil		The Trustee
Al-Qawiyy		The Possessor of All Strength
Al-Matin		The Forceful One
Al-Wali		The Governor
Al-Hamid		The Praised One
Al-Muhsi		The Appraiser

Al-Mubdi'		The Originator
Al-Mu'id		The Restorer
Al-Muhyi		The Giver of Life
Al-Mumit		The Taker of Life
Al-Hayy		The Ever-Living One
Al-Qayyum		The Self-Existing One
Al-Wajid		The Finder
Al-Majid		The Glorious
Al-Wahid		The Unique
Al-Ahad		The Indivisible
As-Samad		The Satisfier of All Needs
Al-Qadir		The All-Powerful
Al-Muqtadir		The Creator of All Power
Al-Muqaddim		The Expediter
Al-Mu'akhkhir		The Delayer
Al-Awwal		The First
Al-Akhir		The Last
Az-Zahir		The Manifest One
Al-Batin		The Hidden One
Al-Wali		The Protecting Friend
Al-Muta'ali		The Supreme One
Al-Barr		The Doer of Good
At-Tawwab		The Guide to Repentance
Al-Muntaqim		The Avenger
Al-'Afuww		The Forgiver
Ar-Ra'uf		The Clement
Malik-al-Mulk		The Owner of All
Dhul-Jalali Wal-Ikram		The Lord of Majesty and Bounty
Al-Muqsit		The Equitable One
Al-Jami'		The Gatherer
Al-Ghani		The Rich One
Al-Mughni		The Enricher
Al-Mani'		The Preventer of Harm
Ad-Darr		The Creator of the Harmful
An-Nafi'		The Creator of Good
An-Nur		The Light
Al-Hadi		The Guide
Al-Badi		The Originator
Al-Baqi		The Everlasting One
Al-Warith		The Inheritor of All
Ar-Rashid		The Righteous Teacher
As-Sabur		The Enduring One

When he was done, he heard Baby Jaan call his name. Muezza climbed down the tree.

'So?' he asked.

'I found the spot where the stores are and dug a tunnel. It's just as you said! Enough supplies for you and me. Till such time as your Shahir fetches you. By the way, I also found some meat in brine, which I washed with some water from the pool and have left on a rock for you,' Baby Jaan said and walked off to sit under a tree.

Muezza loped towards the food and ate till he could eat no more. Then he went towards Baby Jaan, who had strangely gone silent. Something was wrong, he deduced.

'What is it, Baby Jaan?' he asked gently.

'You don't trust me, do you?' she said quietly.

'What do you mean?'

Baby Jaan shook her head. 'You wanted me to be a rat because you thought if I became a dog, I would chase you and harm you . . .'

'The thought did cross my mind,' Muezza admitted, shamefaced. 'Cats don't trust easily!'

'And you think djinns do? But when I became a rat, I didn't think for once that you would hurt me . . . or toy with me before killing me.' Baby Jaan's eyes had a grim expression.

Muezza shuddered. But he also knew a great sense of remorse. She was right. He had to learn to trust.

'I'm sorry, Baby Jaan . . . believe me—I really, truly, sincerely am sorry . . .'

Baby Jaan shrugged but didn't say anything.

'Tomorrow, you choose who you want to be . . . you can be a hound or a giant python or a cauldron of scalding hot water, and I promise I will stand there knowing that you are trustworthy,' Muezza declaimed as he had seen the sahabas do. 'Happy?' he asked, leaning towards her.

'No,' she said. 'I will be happy only if you tell me a story . . . a nice, long story.'

'All right . . .' Muezza agreed with a smile.

'But before that, I have a question,' Baby Jaan interjected. 'My cousin Adam—what happened to him? When did he go back to jannat?'

'Adam's lifespan was supposed to be a thousand years, as I said. However, once when God had shown Adam who his descendants would be, apparently he saw a beautiful light in Prophet Dawud's eyes and knew that he wanted Dawud to live long so he could share his wisdom longer.

'So Adam turned to God and said, "Dear God, please give Dawud forty years from my life."

'God, it is said, smiled and granted Adam his wish. It was written and sealed.

'However, 960 years later when the Angel of Death, Malak al-Maut, came for Adam, he was surprised. The angel reminded him of his gift to Prophet Dawud. But Adam denied it.

'My Shahir says, "Adam denied it and so the children of Adam deny it; Adam forgot and so his children forget; Adam made mistakes and so his children make mistakes . . ."

'God realized that Adam wasn't lying. When you forget, you deny and reject the truth. So God forgave him. Adam then submitted to God's will and his breathing stopped.

'The angels descended, washed the body of the first prophet an odd number of times, dug a grave and buried him. And that's what happened to Adam,' Muezza ended.

'Thank you! I hate stories with open endings . . .' Baby Jaan said.

Muezza smiled. She was a child, he told himself again. For this is the joy of childhood—imagining all loose ends tied, all stories finished.

'And can you start the story now?' Baby Jaan nudged him.

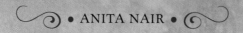

'But I just told you one—' Muezza protested.

'No, you didn't. You just answered my question!' She grinned.

'You tricked me!' Muezza was vexed, but he couldn't resist grinning back.

'I need a nap now. Don't you know you shouldn't tell stories on a full stomach?' He shot her a crafty smile.

'I thought that was said of swimming.'

'Stories, too. So, quiet now and let's grab forty winks . . .'

Muezza curled up into a ball while Baby Jaan sat staring at him helplessly.

15

Muezza had barely entered the phase of deep sleep, in which he'd begin to dream, when he felt something prod his side. He moved without opening his eyes. But the prodding continued.

'What is it, Baby Jaan?' he hissed in exasperation.

'You said forty winks and it's actually ten-times-ten winks you've had!' she hissed back.

Muezza's eyes flew open. Whoever heard of a hissing camel? Actually, whoever heard of a camel that knew multiplication? *Ugh . . .*

'I thought you couldn't count beyond ten,' Muezza said, stretching. It felt good—the arch and pull of the muscles.

'I can't. So each time I reached ten, I started all over again,' Baby Jaan stated, cocking her head and then trying to stretch like a cat.

Muezza opened his mouth to protest but gave up when he saw that Baby Jaan was managing to stretch as well as he did. Maybe it's all in the mind, he thought. Maybe we don't attempt to do things we could just because we have been told we can't.

'So . . .' said Baby Jaan, lying on her side and propping her head up with a leg bent at the joint, 'are we ready to begin?'

'Why do you like stories so much, Baby Jaan?' asked Muezza.

'For they help me understand who I am . . .' she said, choosing her words carefully.

'That's profound.' Muezza frowned. 'I haven't thought about it like that.'

Almost as if to change the subject, Baby Jaan said suddenly, 'Muezza, you said your Shahir is a prophet and you said my cousin Adam is one, too. So how many prophets are there?'

Muezza frowned again. He dragged a claw through his memory, trying to remember. A cat gathered a great deal by sitting quietly. But some memories were buried deep, deep in his head and it wasn't always easy to pounce on the exact answer.

There was a trick to it, though. One just had to try and remember where and how they may have heard it and the memory of the words emerged just as they'd heard them. All of this Muezza did, and suddenly it came to him!

'There are 1,24,000 prophets, of whom 313 are messengers of God. But the first among them was Adam . . . your cousin!' Muezza smiled.

Baby Jaan nodded. It was day and she knew time was running out. Soon his Shahir would come for Muezza and they would have to go their separate ways. Every story Muezza knew, she wanted to know, too.

'Tell me the story about the whale . . . the one you said was as hungry as I am for stories!'

Muezza nodded. 'Yes, that's a good story. I like it, too.'

'Muezza . . .' Baby Jaan said, 'what's a whale?'

Muezza stared at Baby Jaan. The truth was, he didn't know either.

'Umm . . . it's a sea creature,' Muezza made up as he went along. 'With an enormous mouth and a giant belly, and the rest you will understand as I tell you the story of Prophet Yunus.'

'Can you draw me a picture?' Baby Jaan asked suddenly.

'Am I a cat or an artist?' Muezza growled.

'Who said you can't be both?' She batted her eyelids at him as she had seen a girl in the caravan do. Baby Jaan had seen a boy then run to do the girl's bidding at that.

Muezza swallowed. Whenever the female ginger cat at Shahir's home batted her eyelids at him, he wanted to slide up to her and start a conversation. But when Baby Jaan did it, he wanted to screech and dash up the nearest date palm.

'What do I draw with? And where?' he asked, trying to erase that image of Baby Jaan.

'I'll turn into a stick and you can draw on the sand with me,' she said.

'You don't give up, do you?' Muezza sighed.

'My bad . . .' Baby Jaan said, batting her eyelids again.

Muezza grabbed the stick that Baby Jaan had turned into and drew what he thought was a whale. He took great care to emphasize the gigantic mouth and enormous teeth, which were a crucial element in the story. It still didn't seem right so he patted the sand with his paws such that the teeth stood out like real teeth.

When it was done, he stood looking at it carefully, head cocked to one side. The stick turned into a baby camel but he was oblivious to the transformation.

'Wow . . .' a voice said, snapping him out of his thoughts. 'Me likey!'

Muezza grinned and clutched at a stray whisker on his chin thoughtfully. He had seen poets do that. Artists, he presumed, would do the same.

'Right,' he said, pretending not to hear the admiration in the baby camel's exclamation. 'So that's a whale.'

'And now the story?' she said and promptly sat on the whale composition.

'And, yes, now the story,' Muezza repeated and closed his eyes.

It was a trick he had learnt very recently—to narrate a story as if it were playing out before his eyes . . .

The people of a town called Nineveh in the Mosul province were a dissolute lot. They did as they pleased and since the town had been free of wars and natural calamities, they presumed their ways were all right. However, God decided it was time that they were told a few truths. So He guided Prophet Yunus bin Matta to the town of Nineveh.

Yunus arrived on a hot, dry day and called to the people to come hear the message he'd brought—the word of God. Hopeful, Yunus waited at the town square. He was eager to tell them all that he knew. But no one came. And those who did, went away saying they had things to do.

The prophet went to bed disheartened. But he put it down to the heat. Tomorrow would be better, he believed.

The next day was cool and pleasant. But again, no one seemed inclined to hear him. 'Why don't you leave us alone?' they grumbled. 'We and our forefathers have always lived like this. Our gods may not be your god but no harm has come to us. So why should we change our ways?' The prophet was beginning to lose heart and so, after a few days, he decided to leave Nineveh for good.

'There is no point in trying to convince any of you . . . I may as well speak to rocks. You do not heed God's word or the message I bring to you . . .' And then, unable to help himself, Prophet Yunus raised his staff in anger. 'God shall come down on you like a cliff of bricks, a nest of hornets, a series of floods . . . I do not know in what way God will choose to punish you, but do what you are doing and in three days all of you will be dead!'

Prophet Yunus walked away and so great was his rage that he didn't look where he was going. He walked and walked until he arrived at the seashore where he boarded a ship.

Meanwhile, in Nineveh the sky began to change colour and turned hot as fire and red as blood. The people of Nineveh remembered that a prophet named Nuh had warned the people thus and none had listened to him till the Great Flood had happened. So they looked at each other and agreed as one to offer their prayers to God. They climbed a mountaintop and begged for his forgiveness and mercy.

And so God spared them from punishment. The sky turned blue again and the people of Nineveh returned to their homes. They beseeched God to send Prophet Yunus back to them to teach them God's word. But where on earth was Prophet Yunus?

Meanwhile, the ship Yunus was on set sail. Soon a strong wind rose and the clouds turned dark and heavy. The waters churned and the skies split with thunder and lightning. The ship was pounded on all sides by giant waves and it seemed it would capsize and everyone would drown.

The ship began to shudder and shake. People crouched on the deck, clinging to their belongings. But soon the captain of the ship had his men fling the baggage into the sea. But it made no difference. The ship continued to toss about. The waves rose high as hills and then fell as deep as valleys.

And now it was time to do what was done in such circumstances. The weight of the ship had to be further reduced. One by one, a passenger would be thrown off the deck. So lots were drawn and the name of the first person to be thrown into the stormy waters was chosen. The name that appeared was of Yunus.

'No!' the people cried. 'The prophet cannot be thrown into the sea. Let's do it again.'

And so a second lot was drawn. Again the name was of Yunus.

'I don't think I did it right,' the captain protested. 'I got the wrong name. I need to draw lots again.'

But when the prophet's name appeared for the third time, Prophet Yunus knew that this was not a random occurrence. It was God's will. God was angry with the prophet. For he had failed to be patient, and had stormed off in anger without even waiting for God's instructions. Yunus stood on the deck and looked at the angry sea. It was night and there was neither the moon nor the stars. Just a dense blackness and the howling of the wind. Neither Yunus nor his fellow passengers saw the giant shape lurking behind the ship. But Yunus had already made up his mind. So after one last look at the other passengers, he flung himself off the ship and into the sea.

As the passengers watched, a giant whale appeared with its jaws wide open and swallowed him whole. The mouth shut, the long, glistening, ivory teeth snapping in place and looking like fortress gates. And the whale dived to the bottom of the ocean.

When Yunus regained consciousness, he realized that he was in a black,

foul-smelling place. Was this his grave, he wondered. He clambered to his feet and deduced that he was in the belly of a giant fish and that the strong digestive juices inside it were eating away at his skin.

Yunus raised his voice and called out to God. It sounded through the dark space inside the fish, through the dark waters of the sea, through the black of the night . . .

None have the right to be worshipped
But you, O God.
Glorified are you and, truly, I
Have been one of the wrongdoers!

Yunus's call echoed far and beyond till even the angels heard it. They recognized his voice and went to God and said, 'Isn't that Yunus, your righteous servant calling to you in distress?'

God only smiled.

Deep down in the sea, the whale felt the cry echo within it. For a while it was frightened. What have I done, the whale wondered.

Then the whale told itself, 'But I did nothing wrong! I only did what God had asked me to. Swallow the prophet whole!'

Once again at God's command, the giant whale rose to the surface and swam to the farthest end of the ocean where the sun shone and a breeze blew. And again, the whale did as God had asked it to. It swam towards an island and ejected Yunus on to the shore.

Yunus's skin had been eaten away and he cried in anguish, unable to bear the sun and wind. But Yunus continued to call out to God even though his voice was feeble and failing, and he was in agony.

God felt His heart bleed for the prophet and so He caused a vine to grow above him. That was his shelter and source of food.

There Yunus rested till his skin healed and his thoughts came together in a resolve. He knew that he would return to his people and continue the work that God had wanted him to.

When Prophet Yunus returned to Nineveh, he saw that the entire town of 1,00,000 people had gathered to receive him. They told him of all that had happened after he'd gone away.

Filled with gratitude, the prophet fell to his knees—as did the townspeople—and he led a prayer of thanks to God.

'So that's the story of Yunus and the giant fish!' Muezza said, hoping that Baby Jaan had let all the bits of the story sink in.

'What happened to the fish?' Baby Jaan asked.

Muezza smiled. He had known she would ask him that.

'When the fish died, it went to heaven. One of the ten animals who did—' he began, but suddenly shut up, seeing the gleam in Baby Jaan's eyes.

16

Muezza stood up. 'I need to stretch my legs,' he said.

The sun had risen but it wasn't as fiercely hot as it could get in the desert even on a winter's day. Baby Jaan stood up, too.

'Alone!' Muezza frowned. 'Cats need some me-time, Baby Jaan,' he added, seeing her crestfallen face.

'Why?' asked Baby Jaan.

'To think about things. And to just be, without thinking about things,' Muezza said. 'Mostly it's because after a while, cats feel crowded and so we need to take a walk.'

Baby Jaan collapsed on the sand.

Muezza walked without thinking too much about where he was headed. But still, he only walked along the edge of the oasis, afraid to walk out into the desert. He didn't want to get lost again. Two whole nights and almost two days had passed since his Shahir left. Had no one missed him yet?

Muezza looked up to the heavens and called out in prayer. Then he realized that he wasn't in too bad a place. He had food and shelter and a friend. Does a cat need more? Surely not. He would wait it out till his Shahir came for him.

Muezza turned back. This is what he loved about walks. The mind walked, too—squashing the pesky, cockroach-like thoughts, leaping over the puddle-like problems and untangling balls of trouble as if they were twine. Muezza grinned. He was getting very good at this metaphor thing!

Did Baby Jaan know what a metaphor was? He would teach her about it when he got back, he decided.

Suddenly, further up, he saw something that looked like a giant balloon. What on earth was that? He raced towards it. Baby Jaan was on her own there! She would be frightened. Or worse, she would want to make friends with it. And who knew what it was . . .

When Muezza was about a hundred feet away, he stopped and stared in shock. It looked like what he'd drawn on the sand . . . it was a whale! And Baby Jaan was nowhere in sight! Where had the whale come from? Had he conjured it up with his storytelling? And had it swallowed Baby Jaan like it had Prophet Yunus?

Muezza felt his heart thud inside his chest. *What am I going to do? What am I going to do?* he chanted to himself.

Suddenly the whale giggled. 'Gotcha!' it said in a voice that sounded uncannily like Baby Jaan's.

Muezza sat on his haunches, gaping. Was that Baby Jaan? But how had she . . .

'Baby Jaan?' his voice was faint when it emerged.

'You recognized me?' she asked.

Muezza looked at the whale again. He saw that the mouth of the fish was turned up at the corners like Baby Jaan's. Even as a flea, she would have a smiley mouth! He saw the naughty gleam in the whale's eyes.

He nodded. 'How did you manage it? It couldn't have been easy . . .'

The whale shrugged in a way that only whales can. A little tap of the flipper that sent a wave of sand towards Muezza.

'I don't know. I sat on the drawing and began imagining myself as a whale. I had to think very hard and focus, and suddenly I felt my shape shifting. So what do you think?'

Muezza walked closer and examined the whale from all sides. 'You look as you are—a beached whale!'

'Means—'

'Means that you're out of water with no way of moving or breathing . . . whales are not meant to be sitting in the middle of a desert. So you better change shape ASAP!'

'Means?' the whale asked again, trying to wriggle but with little success.

'Means, as soon as possible!' Muezza snorted.

The whale rolled its eyes and in a flash was back to being a baby white camel. Baby Jaan shook herself as if she were a dog.

'Do I smell?' she asked.

'A little . . .' Muezza wrinkled his nose. 'But that's probably because I'm a cat,' he added. 'We are rather fastidious—'

'How does it matter that you're fast?' Baby Jaan asked, rolling in the sand.

'*Fastidious*,' Muezza said, hitting his head with his paw, 'means to be very concerned about matters of cleanliness . . . and not fast in terms of speed.'

'Oh,' Baby Jaan said, giving herself one good roll before standing up on her feet. 'Muezza, while I was a whale, I had a doubt. You said Nuh came before Yunus . . . so who came before Nuh?'

'Hmm . . . Yunus didn't come right after Nuh. There were other prophets between them. But right before Nuh, there was Prophet Idris,' Muezza said.

'Prophet Idris . . . I like the name!' Baby Jaan stated.

'I do, too. And I like the prophet as well.'

'Tell me about him,' insisted Baby Jaan, sliding up to Muezza. 'And no, I'm not asking for a story. I just want to know why you like him.'

Muezza began, 'According to what I have heard, he was a well-built man with a broad chest and a full head of hair. He had a low voice but what he spoke of, drew people to him.

'It is said that God revealed thirty books of thought to Idris and so, to record them, Idris created the pen and thus mankind learnt to write with a pen. Idris also taught people to stitch clothes and how to wear them. The prophet taught people how to gaze at stars and to guide themselves whether they were on land or at sea.'

'Clever,' Baby Jaan said. 'I like him, too. But I have one more question. You said that ten animals are allowed into heaven. So what happens to the rest?'

'They turn to dust.'

'I have one more question . . .' continued Baby Jaan.

'Don't your questions ever end?' Muezza rolled his eyes.

'So who are the other animals, apart from the whale, that get to go to heaven?' Baby Jaan asked, pretending not to have heard him.

'They don't all go to heaven. Just one among them and because of what they did . . .' Muezza replied. He didn't think he would make it to heaven. He wasn't pious enough. Or even truly good. He had stolen fish a few times and even taken a sip from a cauldron of milk when no one had been looking. He had killed a nest of rat babies, and once chased a hen that he later heard had been so frightened that it had become egg-bound.

'Like?' Baby Jaan asked.

'Like the sleepers in the cave and their dog,' Muezza said.

He had wondered about that when he had first heard it, for there was quite a lot of discussion about whether dogs were haram or not. But Muezza had also heard how once when Shahir was leading an army into battle, he had seen a female dog that had just had a litter. So Shahir had posted one of his companions to stand guard over the mother and babies.

'Muezza . . .' Baby Jaan touched his paws. 'Tell me the story.'

Once there was a king who held an annual festival during which everyone gathered to worship idols.

God had forbidden such practices. God didn't want people worshipping what they *thought* was His image. So the followers of the word of God didn't want to be part of the festivities.

The king was a tyrant. When he heard that everyone but a small group of young men would be part of the celebrations, he was angry. His eyebrows, which were like angry caterpillars, grew angrier. His nostrils flared, his mouth became a thin line and he ground his teeth so hard that people in the palace wondered who was grinding grain at midnight. The king ordered for the young men to be seized and killed.

The group of men heard about this and fled. To die for one's faith is the coward's way. To live for one's faith is the noble thing to do and that's what God preached, they realized. To live against all odds and survive—that was the young men's plan.

On their way, they met a young farmer and his dog, Qitmir. The farmer was impressed by the young men's faith and decided to join them. Eventually they reached a cave some distance outside town.

The men entered the cave while Qitmir the dog lay down at its mouth with his legs outstretched, guarding them. When the young men had offered their prayers, God caused them and the dog to fall asleep.

And they slept through year after year. God caused them to turn to their right and left as the sun rose and set, so the sun's rays wouldn't stir them awake. Three hundred and nine years passed this way and yet when the young men and their dog finally woke up, they felt that they had gone to sleep just some hours ago.

The young men stretched and stepped out as the dog barked in short yaps and ran around them, happy to see them.

The men were hungry. So one of them went to the nearest town to buy food with the money they had. There the shopkeeper stared at the ancient silver coin in surprise. Then the story about how they had gone into hiding emerged and soon it spread to all.

The new king was God's follower. So he rushed on foot to see the young men and take their blessings. For surely only God could have made this miracle possible.

When the young men and Qitmir died, they were all buried in the cave. They were together in life and death. And in heaven.

Baby Jaan had a faraway look in her eyes. 'It's such a beautiful story. This Qitmir . . . what did he look like?'

Muezza stretched himself to his full height and crossed his paws at his chest. 'Don't you even think about it! You're going to make yourself ill with all this shape-shifting!'

But Baby Jaan was looking into the horizon with a startled expression.

17

Muezza peered over Baby Jaan's shoulder. What on earth was she looking at? Had the Jaan army returned?

'What is it?' he asked as he scanned the horizon, which, in truth, was a deserted desert and nothing more. It was twilight and the shadows grew tall and fat.

'I can hear panting,' Baby Jaan said thoughtfully.

'You're imagining it . . .' Muezza snorted, wondering if it was time for another meal.

'No, I'm not. I can hear it.'

'Do you see a horse or a hound anywhere?' asked Muezza. 'They are the ones who pant.'

'And the Hinn . . .' Baby Jaan frowned.

'*Hinn?* Who is that now?'

'One of the djinns. Not like us Jaans. They are a weaker lot. And take the form of dogs. A Hinn is around somewhere and, though we may not see it, the Hinn or a band of them will be here soon.'

'Oh,' Muezza said, reflecting. And then, 'Oh,' again for he wasn't sure what they should do.

'Shall I climb up a date palm?' Muezza asked, scampering up a tree even as he spoke. Then he came running down. 'Baby Jaan, I suggest you turn into a cat—then we could both go up to the top of the date palm,' he said, tugging at Baby Jaan.

She shook her head. 'Dogs and cats . . . have you thought of what that means?'

'But we will be on top of the tree! Can the Hinn climb up?' Muezza sounded stupid even to his own ears. But what was that they said—discretion was the better part of valour.

'You really are petrified!' Baby Jaan grinned. 'Hinns can't climb trees but they will circle the date palm and won't leave till we climb down.'

'So what?' Muezza asked thoughtfully.

'It's not them I fear as much as that they will draw the attention of the Jaan army or, worse, the Guls or the Palis . . . and we don't want any of them here,' Baby Jaan said with a grim look.

For the first time, Muezza saw who Baby Jaan would grow up to be. A leader who thought ahead, and on her feet. He could even picture her leading her army of Jaans into battle against the evil Guls and Palis.

'Go crouch in the tunnel that leads to the food cellar. But before doing so, draw circles around it with a stick. Three circles that somehow connect at a single point,' Baby Jaan instructed. 'And when you have finished, place the stick—which will be me—on that point of meeting.'

Muezza said nothing. What was Baby Jaan planning?

'Oh,' she added, 'and take a dip in the pond before you go. I know you hate water but you must.'

Muezza nodded. He knew it was a serious situation. It would soon be night and in the darkness, the powers of djinns became a hundredfold, even of a weak lot like the Hinns.

Muezza looked at the sand for a moment. How was he going to get the circles to connect? Suddenly he knew how. Using the opening of the tunnel as the centre, Muezza drew three intersecting circles with the stick that Baby Jaan had turned into. The sand furrowed into little channels.

Then he went to the pond, took a deep breath and stood there. The stick stood on its end to watch if Muezza would take the plunge. And he did! The stick fell back in relief.

Muezza emerged from the pond, wet, clammy and feeling miserable. But he didn't shake himself as he walked to the mouth of the tunnel.

He was slowly beginning to realize what Baby Jaan had in mind. He entered the opening and, going as far as he could go, crouched there. What would happen next?

Even from under the ground, Muezza could hear an approaching thudding. A pack of dogs, that sounded more like oxen, thundered towards where they were.

When they were about five hundred feet away, Baby Jaan took a deep breath and concentrated hard. The stick burst into flames. And the flames spread to become three blazing circles of fire with flickering red tongues. The Hinns stopped abruptly. Flames in the middle of the desert? Something wasn't right.

Two of the Hinns wanted to investigate. But the leader of the pack was reluctant. 'It's not a real fire . . . I am certain,' he whispered. The tongues of the fire leapt higher. One curled towards them. 'It's something pretending to be something else . . .'

'What do you think we should do?' one of the Hinns asked.

'Turn in the other direction and leave!' the leader said.

'No wonder they call us weak,' the curious Hinns grumbled.

'Well, it's better to walk away from trouble than to court it,' the leader of the pack said, nipping at their legs. 'Now scoot! I don't care if we are called lily-livered djinns . . . I'd rather be lily-livered and alive than be reckless and dead . . .'

The Hinns thundered away and the fire died abruptly. The stick lay smoking as Muezza emerged.

'Baby Jaan,' he whispered. 'You can change shape now. They are gone.'

But the stick continued to lie still, smoking. Muezza waited there, worried. The stick tried to stand on its end but couldn't. Muezza lifted it as if it were a kitten, firmly but tenderly, and took it to the pond. He put his tail into the water and pulled it out when it was wet. Then he gently ran his tail over the stick. Again and again.

The stick sighed and, slowly, it stood upright. And when Muezza blinked, the stick had turned into Baby Jaan again. A tired and spent Baby Jaan, but her white camel self. Whole—and grinning.

'You're braver than brave, Baby Jaan,' Muezza said, not bothering to hide the awe in his voice.

Baby Jaan shrugged. 'I only did what you would do for me,' she replied and stood up to walk away from the pond. She almost buckled, then steadied herself.

Muezza saw that Baby Jaan was limping. 'What's wrong?' he asked.

'Sometimes shape-shifting takes its toll, especially when you play at being fire . . . my great-grandmother is right . . . I know now. She constantly warns me to not play with fire. "You will get burnt," she says. And I think I have burnt myself . . .'

Muezza remembered the smoking stick. One part of it had had an ember stuck to it.

He walked around Baby Jaan and saw that the back of her hind legs had blisters below the joints. The heat had scalded her skin and eaten into the flesh beneath.

'Baby Jaan!' Muezza gasped. 'You must rest and while you do, I will tell you the story of another she-camel who was God's miracle. Just as you are, Baby Jaan . . .'

Muezza thought of that day. He was with Shahir as he rode ahead of the army.

The Byzantine Army, under its emperor Heraclius, was preparing to attack the holy city of Medina. That was when Shahir decided to lead an army of God's followers to save the city. The army comprised 30,000 men, which was

the largest until that time. All of them were God's followers, and they heeded His word as well as what Shahir had brought to them as the message of God.

On his way to this battle, the Battle of Tabuk, Shahir stopped by the dwelling of the Thamud tribe. The people gathered around to meet and speak to him.

They brought the army water to fill their waterskins and kneaded dough for bread that the army could bake to eat. But strangely, Shahir was unhappy. He ordered the army to empty out the waterskins and give the bread to the camels to eat. Then he led his men towards a well some distance away.

'I fear that you will be afflicted by what afflicted them,' he began.

And then he told them about Prophet Salih and the she-camel.

18

'The city of Iram was a beautiful land. Caravans that ran between India and places north of the Arabian peninsula stopped here and so the city prospered. But there was more to their welfare. The people of Iram knew how to produce frankincense and they became the distributors of this wondrous resin that forms on trees—'

Baby Jaan blinked. 'What is this frankincense?' She nudged Muezza. 'Do you know what it is? Does one eat it?'

Muezza thought of how, in the early evenings, little bits of frankincense would be flung on a pan of coals. A fragrant smoke would waft up and fill the rooms. But he hadn't seen anyone eat it. 'It's used to make a room fragrant,' he explained.

'Oh, but why would anyone need to make a room fragrant?' Baby Jaan asked, sniffing the air. The cold desert air of the night smelled of nothing.

'Do you want to debate smells or do you want me to tell you the story?' Muezza snapped in annoyance. A storyteller ought to be allowed to tell his story without being interrupted, he thought. Or, he would lose his flow.

'Sorry . . .' Baby Jaan said in a small voice. She thought of her eazima and figured out the use of the resin.

Muezza cleared his throat and began again.

The people of Iram, or the people of 'Ad as they were referred to, were rich. They built buildings on all the high places, each one finer than the other. They believed that their tribe and their homes would live forever. They forgot the teachings of God and, instead, worshipped idols, whom they called Samd,

Samud and Hara. And as their riches grew, they became cruel and devious.

Meanwhile, a child was born and at the time of his birth, his mother had visions that convinced her that there was only one God. The child was named Hud and he grew up worshipping God. And when it was time, God wished him to speak to the people of 'Ad about the evil of their ways.

Prophet Hud, who was a fourth-generation descendant of Nuh, tried very hard to convince them to forswear their false gods and seek out the true God. But their riches made them both arrogant and brutish.

'Go away,' they cried. 'We see no reason to believe you . . . you are but a prophet of gloom . . . *don't do this, don't do that!*'

'Chew on a chicken leg and you'll feel less *gloooomyyy!*' one of them mocked him.

But Prophet Hud did his best. He continued to preach and they continued to mock him. The prophet didn't lose heart, though. 'God has given you all you have—cattle and sons, gardens and springs—but there will come a day when you will have to pay a great penalty. It's still not too late . . .' he pleaded with them.

A few asked him to shut up. 'This is the customary device of the ancients! To try and frighten us with stories of pain and penalty,' they said.

And a heckler called out, 'Go take a bath . . . maybe that will help you forget all this nonsense! And throw in a handful of bay leaves. That will clear your mind!'

Prophet Hud buried his head in his hands. 'What shall I do, my God? I have tried to show them again and again the errors of their ways.'

'Why do you look unhappy?' a little child walked up to him and asked.

'I have tried to tell the people of 'Ad that if they continue to be as they are—cruel, wilful and lacking in mercy—God will eventually seek them out and make them pay . . . but no one is bothered. None will listen.'

The little child took his hand in his. 'I will, Prophet Hud.'

The prophet smiled. He had conveyed his message to someone. And if even a child could grasp its truth, the people of 'Ad were surely being obstinate in rejecting it.

That evening, a cloud gathered over the land. A few people wondered if it was the storm that Hud had prophesied.

'It's just a passing cloud,' they said. 'It will bring us rains and make our gardens greener, our springs fuller, our cattle plumper and our sons stronger! So much for that nutcase, Hud, and his prophecies of doom.'

A wind rose but no rains came. Instead sand swirled and whirled. For seven nights and eight days, the wind raged and howled. The people were struck down, one by one, as though they were hollowed-out palm trees. They lay there devastated and decimated by the wind that showed them no mercy.

When the storm ceased, the people of 'Ad had been wiped out. Their fine homes and buildings atop tall places, their gardens and their parks were all empty. It was as if the people of 'Ad had never existed.

Baby Jaan yawned.

'What? You didn't like my story?' Muezza was most affronted.

Baby Jaan yawned again. 'I liked it, but you'd said that you were going to tell me a story about a camel, a miracle camel. Where was the camel?'

Muezza winced; he had thought he would build up the drama before leading to the story of the camel. But it seemed to not have worked as he had hoped. He wasn't going to admit that, though. Everyone was a critic these days—even baby camels who were wet behind the ears—and he saw no reason to give them opportunities to nit-pick.

Instead he growled. 'Did I tell you that the story was over? You need to be patient, Baby Jaan . . .'

19

The people of 'Ad had been decimated for their wanton ways. And in their place, the tribe of Thamud had come to be. The debris of destruction was swept away and the Thamud people revived the glory of the land. They became rich and powerful and, once again, their gardens grew green; their cattle, plump; their springs ran full and their children grew strong. They built tall buildings in the plains and carved out beautiful homes in the hills. It would have been a blessed land except, like the people of 'Ad, the Thamud, too, grew arrogant with all their power and grandeur.

And like the people of 'Ad, they took to worshipping false gods. The strong dominated the weak. The oppressors lost all vestiges of kindness and instead ruled with a brutal hand. Not even a bee could buzz unless they said so.

So God decided to send a prophet to them as well. He chose a person from among the people, who was called many names—Salih ibn Ubeid, Ibn Maseh, Ibn Ubeid, Ibn Hader, Ibn Thamud, Ibn Ather, Ibn Eram and Ibn Noah.

Everyone loved Prophet Salih at first. They saw in him someone who was both wise and good, and with purity of intent. But when Salih began speaking to them about God, they shook their heads in dismay.

But Salih persisted. He went to their stately buildings in the plains and their fine homes in the hills. He stood in the town square and in the gardens. 'My people,' he said. 'Worship God; there is no other god but Him.'

The people grew angry. The prophet and his revelations from God weren't what they wanted to hear.

'Until you came to us with this new thing, we were actually considering making you our leader . . . but now we are not so sure! You want us to stop worshipping the gods our fathers did and instead worship this god you talk about! Why should we? Go away . . .'.

But Salih wouldn't be dissuaded. Soon they began suspecting he was mad. Only a madman would rave and rant like this, contrary to everything that everyone else believed.

The people gathered around him one day and said, 'Tell you what . . . this god that you speak of . . . we'll accept your word if you get your god to perform a miracle.'

Prophet Salih frowned. Nevertheless he agreed.

Together the people went to the place chosen by them. It was high up in the hills and strewn with rocks and boulders. There they pointed at a rock and said, 'Ask your god to bring forth a camel from that giant rock!'

Salih looked at them and asked, 'Anything else?'

'Yes, it must be a she-camel, ten months pregnant, tall and attractive.'

Salih nodded. 'And when God makes that happen,' he asked, 'will you believe what I have been saying all along and accept it as truth?'

'Yes.' They smirked. When you crack open a rock, you get a rock, not a camel. Even a moron knew that!

Then God sent forth a thunderbolt that crashed through the skies and descended on the giant rock with a sound that brought the people to their knees. The boulder split into two and out of it stepped a beautiful she-camel, tall and stately and ten months pregnant.

Here was the miracle they had sought. It was a wondrous sight and many of the people gathered there called out to the heavens and declared their faith in God. The she-camel walked towards the plains and there it lived amidst people.

One afternoon the she-camel drank from a well, and drank and drank and drank till it seemed that there would be no water left. The people looked at each other, dismayed and angry. 'What are we going to do?' they demanded, raising their clenched fists at Prophet Salih.

'Be patient,' he said.

Soon milk began to flow from the camel's udders. So much milk, that it was enough for all the people of Thamud! Men, women and children drank their fill, and there was still enough and more.

Where the she-camel rested at night, no other beast would dare go. So the people found it safe to be where she was.

The she-camel that was a blessing from God roamed freely, drinking water from her favourite well, grazing amidst cattle and seeking a quiet place at night to rest. God's followers were happy but there were many who weren't.

In fact, the hatred they felt for Salih was now directed towards the she-camel.

'She's drinking up all our water!'

'She's frightening the cattle!'

'She roams through the gardens, mucking them up!'

'The other day I saw her spitting into the stream!'

'Just yesterday she almost bit my daughter!'

Every day they had a new complaint. And day by day their hatred grew.

So they hatched a plan. Two young men were promised two girls from noble families as their brides if they killed the she-camel.

The men, Masarai and Quadir, were tempted. It was a dream come true for them. How else could they find such beautiful brides? They were very ordinary young men and they didn't have much to recommend them. So they followed the she-camel for a few days; they watched her every move and what she ate and where she lay.

One warm day, the she-camel was thirsty and she went to the well she liked to drink from. It was a blessed well for under the ground was a spring that filled it with water even as it was emptied. The she-camel knew about this and so she sought this well, knowing that the more she drank from it, the more it would be replenished. But still she'd wait for the people to fetch the water they needed from her favourite well first. That afternoon, when everyone was resting, Masarai and Quadir followed the she-camel as she went to the well again.

Masarai crept up behind her without making a sound, his bow strung and ready, and in it, an arrow. He shot the arrow into her leg. Immediately, the she-camel felt something pierce her. The arrow had struck the hamstring of her leg and the pain was excruciating. She knew that there was danger lurking and tried to escape, but she was hobbling with pain and that was when Quadir raised his sword and cut her other leg from behind.

The she-camel fell to her knees and then Quadir raised his sword again, this time to pierce her heart. The she-camel died instantly and a curious stillness settled over the hills and plains.

But Masarai and Quadir whooped in triumph, breaking the stillness. When they returned to tell the non-believers what they had done, they were received like heroes. Songs were sung, drums beaten and pipes played. The people mocked Salih, 'Where's your she-camel? Where's your she-camel? If your god sent her, why didn't your god watch out for her?'

Salih felt his throat choke with tears at their cruelty. But even though tears flowed down his cheeks, he tried once again to tell them that they were wrong in doing what they had done. But they pushed him away. 'Shut up! We'll put you down like we did your she-camel.'

The prophet stared at them for a long moment. In a quiet voice, he said, 'Enjoy the time left to you. In three days, God's wrath will descend upon you!'

'Why three days? Why not now?' They laughed in his face.

Salih pleaded with them. 'Don't . . . please don't do this . . . you are hastening the horrors that will befall you . . .'

'Horrors, you say?' They booed him. 'You and your horrible followers are the horrors we have had to endure. That she-camel of yours . . . was it even a camel or a creature brought to ruin us?'

Salih walked away. That night he had a revelation. God asked him to leave with his followers. The people of Thamud were planning to murder him. But God also wanted him and his followers to leave for another reason.

On the third day, as Prophet Salih had said would happen, thunderbolts tore up the skies while earthquakes shook the land. Everything that was stately and fine, crumbled; every living creature died and the entire tribe of Thamud was no more.

'So you understand why I compared you to the blessed she-camel who went to heaven?' Muezza grinned. 'But wait—why do you look like I do when I find the cream and eat it all up?'

Baby Jaan snorted. 'Did a cat ever get to heaven? I'm just happy to know that my cousin is in jannat . . .' Baby Jaan mused, her eyes round with awe.

'So she is your cousin now?' Muezza drawled.

'Yes, of course!' Baby Jaan said, standing up. 'Look at me, am I not tall and stately?'

Muezza rolled his eyes. 'Yes, you are,' he said in a faint voice. 'How is your leg?' he asked.

'It hurts less now. Maybe if you tell me just one more story, it will heal completely,' Baby Jaan insisted, pretending to look as innocent as possible. 'Your stories have healing powers, Muezza,' she added softly.

'Do you realize that it is late in the night?' Muezza said. 'Don't camels need to sleep?'

Baby Jaan shrugged.

'Well, cats need to. We spend a great deal of time sleeping and, as you know, I cannot function without my catnaps. So, goodnight.'

20

At dawn, the two of them woke up and went for a little walk. Muezza was deep in thought. He walked staring at the horizon.

Baby Jaan looked at him curiously. He seemed to be in a strange mood. 'What's wrong, Muezza?' she asked.

'It's our third dawn since we've been in the desert. What if Shahir never comes back?' he said in a low voice as they walked back. The sky was a brilliant blue and the heat curled around them like a heavy sheepskin. But in the oasis, there was relief. And by the pool, it was pleasant enough. A little breeze came in from somewhere, ruffling the surface of the water into little waves.

'Do you think that will happen?' Baby Jaan asked gently. 'Don't you have faith in your Shahir?'

'I do . . . but doubts are like shadows. When the light is behind you, they loom larger than you. And so every step you take, you're walking into your own shadow.'

'I don't understand.' Baby Jaan frowned. 'How is the light behind you? Look, the sun has just risen!'

'Never mind.' Muezza sighed and got up to go. He'd climb a tree and scan the distance. Maybe if he sat there and willed it, he would see what he wanted. A speck on the horizon.

But even though Muezza sat there till the sun had begun its descent in the skies, the horizon stayed undisturbed. Starting to grow hungry, he climbed down. He went looking for Baby Jaan but there was no sign of her. For the first time, Muezza was truly afraid. Had she gone away, too? She had come like the wind into his life and she could very well leave with the same casual ease of a breeze . . .

'Baby Jaan!' he called. 'Baby Jaan, where are you?'

A little cluster of dates from the tree he had been sitting on fell at his feet.

'Gotcha-mutcha!' The date cluster chortled and then danced a silly jig. Muezza thought his jaw would drop to the ground. What on earth!

In a flash, the date cluster turned into Baby Jaan before he could even take a good look.

'You didn't think I was going to let you walk off on your own, did you?' Baby Jaan said. 'What if you dozed off on top of that tree and fell down?'

'You're not my mother!' Muezza growled.

'I'M YOUR FRIEND. AND FRIENDS WATCH OUT FOR EACH OTHER!' Baby Jaan hollered.

Muezza sat up in shock. 'All right . . . but you don't need to shout!' Then he began to walk away.

'Where are you going?' she asked, wondering if he was angry with her.

'Are you hungry?' he asked.

Baby Jaan nodded.

'I'm going to the cellar. Is there something there you would like to eat?'

Baby Jaan nodded again. 'I think there's a bag of dry fruits there that I wouldn't mind . . . apricots and raisins, figs and twigs . . .'

Twigs? Was she serious? Baby Jaan was going through a rhyming phase, Muezza decided, shaking his head in amusement.

When they had eaten their fill, and Baby Jaan felt like the blessed she-camel must have after a drink from the well, Baby Jaan crouched alongside Muezza and said, 'And now for a story about one of the other blessed animals! We've had the whale and the dog and my cousin . . . Who will it be now?'

Muezza smiled. 'The heifer . . .'

There was an old prophet called Ibrahim. One evening, three angels called Jibril, Mika'il and Israfil went to visit him, disguised as three young men, handsome and strong. They knocked on his door. Ibrahim had never seen them before but something about their bearing made him think they were not who they were pretending to be.

But that didn't matter to Ibrahim for all guests, young or old, rich or poor, man or woman, were welcome in his home. He seated them and went quietly into the inner room. The young men looked tired and hungry and it was his duty, as their host, to take care of their needs even though they were strangers.

In the kitchen he found that his wife Sarah and the maid Hajar had been cooking but there was no choice dish. So he looked among his animals and chose the plumpest of heifers. His pet one, in fact. The heifer looked at Ibrahim sadly, for he'd believed his master loved him. But Ibrahim slaughtered the heifer for he knew his guests came first. Soon the meat was roasted over hot coals. He had it arranged on his finest platter and brought it towards them, placing it at arm's reach.

'Will you not eat?' the prophet asked politely and kindly, for that is how a good host venerates his guest. Instead of asking, he offers.

Jibril, Mika'il and Israfil didn't move. Ibrahim trembled within. *Who were they*, he wondered.

'Don't be afraid.' They smiled.

'What are you here for?' Ibrahim asked.

The young men's expressions turned graven. 'We have come to punish criminals. To bring down upon them a rain of stones. Each one has his or her name written on that piece of clay. We have been sent here to punish the people who live in the place that Lut does.'

Ibrahim's wife, who was standing there, nodded. The people mentioned *were* wicked and vile and transgressed against God again and again. It was exactly what they deserved.

They turned to Ibrahim's wife and said, 'We bring you news, too—good news. You will soon be the mother of sons.'

Ibrahim's wife struck herself on her forehead. 'But how is that possible? For I am an old woman and my husband is an old man. My childbearing years are long gone . . . and even when I was a young woman, I was barren.'

The young men smiled. 'God knows best and God wills it so.'

Prophet Ibrahim and his wife were overjoyed but he was suddenly struck by the thought of what was going to happen to Lut. He decided he would raise the subject, though by now he'd realized that these were no ordinary men.

'Can't Lut and his people be spared?' Ibrahim asked.

The divine messengers' faces darkened. But in a gentle voice, they said, 'What God has decided upon cannot be reversed. So abandon that thought. God created everything in pairs—heaven and earth, night and day, sun and

moon, land and sea, light and darkness, death and life, faith and disbelief, misery and happiness, and thus animals, plants and all life. Only God is one. And those who forget that have to pay!'

Ibrahim's mouth fell open. 'But Lut lives there, with the people!'

'Yes, but Lut and his family will be spared. Not his wife, though. The land they live on will turn into a dead sea where nothing will thrive.'

And so it happened.

As for the heifer who had been sacrificed for the angels, as reward it was blessed and taken to jannat to be with the other blessed animals.

'And were the children born to Ibrahim?' Baby Jaan asked.

Muezza grinned. 'Yes, and there is a blessed animal in that story, too.'

'Oh! What animal was that?' Baby Jaan asked. 'Let me guess . . . a goat!'

'Almost . . .' Muezza said.

'What do you mean *almost*? Tell me!'

Prophet Ibrahim had two sons. His firstborn was from his maid Hajar, whom he married, and the other from his wife Sarah.

After a while, Ibrahim settled Hajar and their son, Ismail, in an arid valley in Arabia. It was surrounded by hills and mountains on all sides that would protect them. He seated them under a tree, and left a bag of dates and some water for them. Before he left, he prayed to God to take care of Hajar and his infant son as they were alone and had little to themselves.

One day, Hajar discovered that there was hardly any food and water left. How would they survive till Ibrahim returned?

In her desperation, Hajar went this way and that, looking for water. She kept running back and forth between Mount Safa and Mount Marwah. Each time she would think, *did I miss checking that part of the ground? Did I peek behind the bush? Did I lift that stone? What if the water source was under that stone?* She had done this seven times already when she saw Ismail kick the ground with his heel. And suddenly a spring of water gushed out and they were saved.

When the prophet returned, he was amazed to see the valley transformed. It was green and fertile. Hajar had died and Ismail was a grown man; and Ibrahim knew that his son was not just any child but one who was special. Ibrahim hugged Ismail as if he would never let him go. He felt remorse for having missed out on his son's childhood but God had decreed it and Ibrahim did whatever God wanted him to.

One day, Ibrahim summoned his son and announced, 'My son Ismail! God wants me to perform a task.'

Ismail said, 'You must do whatever God wants you to.'

Ibrahim put an arm around his son and asked softly, 'Will you help me?'

Ismail hugged his father and murmured, 'Whatever you want me to do, I will.'

And so, assembling stones, father and son built the Kaaba with their own hands.

Some years later, Ibrahim had a strange dream one night. He dreamt that God told him to sacrifice Ismail. The prophet woke up sweating profusely. He was quite sure that it was Iblis whispering in his ear, causing the bad dream.

But the next night Ibrahim had the terrible dream again. This time, he woke up with a heavy heart. He knew God would ask him to sacrifice his son only for a very good reason. Ibrahim loved his son more than his own life and so would have offered his life instead, but God wanted Ismail and no one else.

The next day, Ibrahim asked Ismail to go with him to Mount Arafat. He took along a knife and some rope. Ismail wondered what his father needed them for but didn't ask. On their way, they passed a place called Mina. Iblis had been waiting there and sneaked up behind Ibrahim to sow seeds of doubt in his mind. But Ibrahim walked on and so did Ismail.

When they reached Mount Arafat, Ibrahim sat Ismail down and told him of his dream and what God wanted him to do.

Ismail accepted his fate. He said, 'Abba, I suggest you tie my hands and legs and blindfold me, so I won't see what is about to happen and don't struggle against it. You must cover your eyes, too, so you are not upset by what you have to do.'

Ibrahim looked at his exceptional son sadly. His heart was breaking but he did as Ismail asked. Then he took the knife and did as God had asked him to. But when he removed the cloth wound around his eyes, in the place of his son, he saw a dead ram! And Ismail standing at his side.

God spoke to the prophet, assuring him that all was well. That this was a test and that both Ibrahim and Ismail had sincerely declared their faith.

'So the ram also went to jannat,' Muezza finished.

Baby Jaan leaned towards Muezza. 'Tell me something. Do only animals that have been part of the lives of prophets go to jannat?'

Muezza raised an eyebrow in amusement. 'It does sound like that, doesn't it?'

'Yes . . .' Baby Jaan said.

'Well, you're wrong . . . take the story of the cow!'

'Oh, what was that story?' Baby Jaan asked in her most disinterested voice.

21

Among the children of Israel was an old man whose vault was filled with so many precious jewels that it was impossible to count. A man could count all through his lifetime and he would die without having gone through even one-ninth of it. The old man's nephews wanted the wealth for themselves but they were reluctant to wait for the time of the old man's demise when it would all be theirs. There came a day when one nephew decided he could wait no longer.

He stole into his uncle's home and as the old man lay fast asleep in his bed, the nephew strangled him. Then he took the old man's body and threw it on the road. When it was dawn, the corpse was found by a few people and soon more people gathered. The nephews came running. They saw their dead uncle and began to weep and weep. The nephew who had murdered him wept so much that there was a puddle of tears at his feet.

He looked around at his cousins and demanded, 'Which one of you killed my uncle? Tell me, which one of you did it?'

All the nephews looked at each other suspiciously. All of them stood to gain from it, but who had been the one to commit the crime? They began beating each other up.

'If anyone knows anything about this murdered man, speak now,' the townspeople said.

But none of the nephews owned up to the crime. Instead they pulled out their swords.

Then a few others gathered around and, seeing the fight turn ugly, intervened. 'We suggest you go to the prophet Musa.'

So they went to Prophet Musa and told him that their uncle had been murdered but no one knew who had done it. 'Ask your god to help us,' they pleaded.

The prophet asked his God. When he returned after his prayers, he said, 'My God asks you to slaughter a cow.'

The nephews glared at the prophet. 'Are you making fun of us?'

'My God says you are to slaughter a cow.'

'Why a cow? Why not a camel or a horse? What's so special about a cow? After all, a cow is a cow . . .' the nephews growled in annoyance.

'Did I say just any cow?' Musa asked quietly.

'What other kind is there?' The guilty nephew smirked. Musa was an old fraud, he decided. He wondered if he should bribe the prophet to point out one of his cousins as the murderer.

'Listen to me,' the prophet said in his sternest voice. 'It must be a cow that's trained neither to till the soil nor water the fields; and it should be no other colour but bright yellow. It can neither be young nor old.'

The nephews wondered if the old prophet was mad but they also knew that the people of the town would have all of them punished if the guilty man was not found.

So they wandered far and wide, east and west, north and south, up and down, ran around in circles and took the untrodden path. Till they finally found such a cow owned by a man who was good and treated his old parents with respect and dignity. He worked hard all day and he divided all his earnings into three parts: one part for his parents, one part for charity and one part for himself. The nephews tried to buy the cow from him but he refused. They kept increasing the asking price till they offered ten times the weight of the cow in gold. Finally the man accepted the offer and the nephews led the cow to the prophet.

'Now slaughter it!' the prophet said.

So the cow was slaughtered though the nephews were reluctant to, keeping in mind the price they had paid for it.

'Now take the thigh bone of the dead cow and strike the body of your uncle with it,' the prophet commanded.

They did as he asked and God willed for the old man to come back to life. The nephews stepped back in shock.

'Now tell us, old man, who amongst your nephews was the one to do you harm?' Musa asked.

The old man pointed to his murderer. 'He is the one,' he said in a voice that was filled with sadness, for that nephew had been his favourite.

Then he lay down on the ground and closed his eyes. And God willed him to die again. The all-hearing, all-seeing God had wanted the people to know that He had the power to give as well as to take.

'What do you think of this story?' Muezza asked.

'I like it; but why did the cow have to die?' Baby Jaan said sadly.

'Well, she was one of the blessed animals. And so her place in jannat was certain for it had been planned that she would be God's instrument to demonstrate a truth.'

'I guess. Tell me about this Prophet Musa . . . is he your cousin? You have the same name!' Baby Jaan asked, wondering if they were one and the same. Muezza the cat could very well be a prophet; he seemed to know everything.

'Hardly.' Muezza sighed. 'Whatever you think, I'm not prophet material.'

Baby Jaan gaped. How had Muezza read her mind again?

'I'm just an ordinary cat . . .' he mewed softly. 'I'm a cat. I kill rats. I use my paws to pat. I always fall flat—on my feet no matter how high I am—I don't know what fear is . . . *ahem* . . . for I am a cat. Just a regular, meow-meow kitty-cat!'

'You sing, too!' Baby Jaan said, taking up the song.

Muezza winced. Her voice was like a piece of metal being dragged on the ground; it made the hair on his neck stand on end.

'Stop, stop!' he implored.

'Don't you like my singing?' she asked in a hurt voice.

'It's lovely.' Muezza shuddered. 'But cats and djinns shouldn't sing. We should leave that to the birds . . .'

'Birds! Yes . . . birds are nice. Tell you what, I will stop singing,' Baby Jaan assured him. 'But you need to tell me a story. A story about a bird!'

Muezza smiled. He had a bird story all right. *Ready, steady, go*, he told himself.

22

King Suleiman of Jerusalem was not just any other king. He was wise and good and worshipped God from the core of his being. And as he knew the language of birds, insects and animals, he also consulted them to help him rule better.

Among his bird councillors was the hoopoe. The hoopoe had a rare ability. God had granted him the instinct to see and identify sources of underground water no matter how barren the land was. And so when Suleiman and his army set out, the hoopoe was their water diviner; and no matter where they went, they would have water. All they had to do was dig it up.

One day Suleiman wanted to discuss a certain matter with the hoopoe. But the hoopoe was nowhere to be found.

'Where is the hoopoe?' the king demanded.

But no one knew.

'Is it that he's here and I cannot see him?' he thundered.

But the hoopoe couldn't be found.

'If the hoopoe isn't here soon, I will have to punish him!' The king was more furious than anyone had ever seen him. Everyone turned white with shock. They had seen the king gesture with his hand the slicing of his throat. The hoopoe would be killed if he didn't have a good reason for absenting himself.

'Muezza,' Baby Jaan prodded him, 'why was King Suleiman so angry? Wasn't the hoopoe his friend?'

'Kings don't have friends, Baby Jaan,' Muezza said. 'They cannot if they have to be just. Or they would be accused of having favourites.'

'Still . . .' Baby Jaan grumbled.

'If the king made an exception for the hoopoe, then the lion and the monkey, the heron and the eagle would all expect favours, too.'

Baby Jaan nodded though she wasn't sure about Muezza's point of view. Not really.

'And then?' she asked. She wanted to know what happened to the hoopoe.

And then there was a flutter of wings. The hoopoe flew in and perched on his seat.

King Suleiman glared at him. 'You are late. Where were you?'

'Patience, King,' the hoopoe said. Everyone gasped. This was a mighty king and he was only a little bird even if he had a little crown on his head. The king smiled secretly, though. He had always known that the hoopoe would have a reason for staying away.

'I come to you with intelligence like you have never heard before. I've got to know that which you do not; and I have come to you from Saba with exciting news.'

The king leaned forward. As did the entire court. 'And what may that be?' the king asked.

'I found a woman ruling over the land of Saba and she has everything that could be possessed by a ruler on earth—and, King Suleiman, she has a great throne!' the hoopoe said in a rush and then had to pause to catch his breath.

'Who is this?' King Suleiman demanded.

'Queen Bilquis . . . she is as beautiful as her throne and as strong as any man could hope to be,' the hoopoe said.

'You seem besotted by her!' King Suleiman's eyes twinkled.

'She is a fine woman, but . . .' The hoopoe's head dropped.

'But?'

'But she and her people do not worship God. Instead they worship the sun. Iblis has ensured that they believe what they do is right. They cannot see God for Iblis has blinded them,' the hoopoe explained.

The king said nothing and retired to his chambers. He sent for the hoopoe in private.

'Tell me about this Queen Bilquis,' King Suleiman commanded as soon as the hoopoe flew in to sit on his habitual perch in the king's chamber.

The hoopoe cleared his throat and began, 'When the king of Saba died, he had no sons to ascend the throne as the next king. But he had a daughter who had been well trained by him in kingship. She was very intelligent and an eager learner; soon there was only little she didn't know. However, the people of Saba appointed a man as king. It was the worst decision ever made. He was a wicked man and under his regime, the kingdom was plagued with the troubles he caused. Bilquis knew it was time to step in. She asked the new king to marry her. He happily agreed for now his claim as being king would be questioned by no one.

'On their wedding night, she offered him the choicest of wines. And when he was drunk, she beheaded him and hung his head from the handle of the door. And thus she became the queen of Saba with a strong army and a prosperous kingdom. This is the story of Bilquis. She is the smartest woman on earth. There is nothing she doesn't know. So it will not be easy to convince her about God. She is God's chosen one even though she doesn't know it.'

King Suleiman had been listening carefully. He sat down at his writing table and wrote Queen Bilquis a letter.

'Take this to her and make sure that she and only she reads this,' he said to the hoopoe when he had finished. And so the hoopoe flew straight to the kingdom of Saba, which was far away.

The hoopoe knew it wasn't going to be easy getting an audience with the queen. Her guards kept a close vigil so that no harm could come to her. Everyone adored her and they wouldn't allow even the smallest of threats anywhere near her. The hoopoe knew he would be shot down if they spied him. Or that if the message he carried fell into the wrong hands, it would never reach the queen. Either way, the mission would not be accomplished. So he waited until, one day, he had the perfect opportunity.

Queen Bilquis was sitting at her window, gazing at the flowers in her garden. The hoopoe chose that moment to fly towards the window. He waited till the queen's maids had left the room and then he dropped the letter near her so she would see it.

Queen Bilquis saw the scroll delivered by the bird and picked it up, astonished. What a strange messenger, she thought, and who could the message be from?

She unfurled the scroll and read its contents. King Suleiman had written, asking her and her subjects to become God's followers.

The hoopoe waited to see what the queen would do. She called her statesmen and ministers and told them of the letter.

'It has come from the noble king Suleiman. Tell me what to do. As you know, whatever I do is done only after consulting you.'

The statesmen scratched their foreheads and tugged at their beards. 'We are very well prepared for war, if that's what you want. We'll go with whatever you decide.'

Queen Bilquis didn't want to go to war. She knew King Suleiman was someone who couldn't be fooled, deceived or resisted. And if they went to war, the land would be destroyed and, in all probability, she would be punished with death. But she saw no reason to become God's follower either. If there was such a god, he needed to make it obvious to her that she didn't know everything as she believed she did.

So the queen thought she would win King Suleiman's goodwill by sending him presents. Most kings just needed to know that they had made a point.

Perhaps that would be enough for him, too, and then he wouldn't insist on her and her people becoming God's followers, she told herself. That way, peace would be preserved.

But King Suleiman laughed at the gifts. He said to her chief messenger, 'I don't need any of this. These riches are nothing compared to what I have been given by God.

'Please tell your queen that we are not to be provoked. And tell her to not make us come to your land and force a meeting. All we want is to tell your queen who God is and why we must worship Him. For there is a God beyond the sun you worship.'

The chief messenger and his retinue rushed back to Saba where Queen Bilquis was waiting. She saw the approaching horses and her heart leapt into her mouth.

What had King Suleiman said?

23

'I like this Queen Bilquis, Muezza,' Baby Jaan said. 'She sounds strong but not arrogant . . . one day, when I am queen, I want to be like her!'

Muezza smiled and stretched. He was beginning to see the point of stories. It made the listener introspect; think ahead or look back. It made him think, too . . . that the storyteller has to be careful.

'What are you thinking about?' Baby Jaan peered into his face.

'Stories.' Muezza's voice was soft.

'Are you falling asleep?' Baby Jaan blew into his face.

Muezza sat up with a start. 'What are you doing?'

'Waking you up! Tell me what happened next. What did Queen Bilquis say? What did Queen Bilquis do?'

Queen Bilquis received the message in silence. She was both intrigued and apprehensive. Going to war was the easiest decision for a ruler to make, especially if the ruler was supported by an able army and a court of loyalists. What was more difficult was to negotiate peace without losing face in front of her people or buckling under the demands of the other ruler. Queen Bilquis decided to go meet King Suleiman in person. And she would then decide what she must do, she told herself as she called the court to announce her decision. The hoopoe, who had come back to Saba to see what happened next, returned to King Suleiman.

King Suleiman was sitting with the people of Banu Israel, busy as he was with ruling the land from dawn to noon, when suddenly there was a flutter of wings. The king looked up in surprise to see the hoopoe.

'The . . . queen is o-on her . . . way-to-see-you!' the hoopoe informed. His words issued in fits and bursts as he had flown non-stop and was very, very, very tired.

'Do they come to me in war or in peace?' the king asked.

'In peace, my king. The queen wants to know you better, I think. She is a wise woman. Knows that there is no real victory in war. That both the victor and the vanquished suffer—this is what I heard her say.'

The king smiled. He was eager to meet Queen Bilquis, too. But he wanted to test her first. He looked at the djinns present there and declared, 'I would like her throne brought to me ahead of her arrival.'

A robust djinn leapt up and said, 'I will bring it to you before you rise from the council! In fact, it will be here even before, getting weary of staring at a point, you blink—'

'Go then, djinn,' King Suleiman commanded. 'But do make sure you bring it as it is, without a single gem lost or a tarnish on its beauty or a scratch on its side.'

And so the throne was brought. Then King Suleiman called his workmen and had it altered, disguising it in a way that the queen wouldn't recognize it.

'Why do you do this, King?' the hoopoe asked.

'So that I can know if she's guided by God even though she doesn't know it. Clarity of thought is God's blessing, hoopoe.'

Soon the queen and her attendants arrived. She was taken to the guest chamber prepared for her, and there she sat on the disguised throne. The queen looked at it, puzzled, but didn't speak.

Then one of King Suleiman's councillors came to her and asked, 'Is something the matter?'

The queen smiled and replied, 'It is this throne . . .'

The councillor queried, 'What's wrong with the throne, Queen? Do you know this throne?'

The queen nodded. Then she said, 'It is mine. I would know my throne no matter how well it has been disguised. But how did my throne, which I left behind in Saba, reach Jerusalem? Who could have achieved this marvellous feat?'

The queen received no answers but all day and night she thought about it.

Meanwhile, King Suleiman prepared another test for her. In his royal hall, the king created a *sarh*, beyond which he sat on his throne, waiting to receive her.

'Wait, Muezza, tell me what a sarh is!' Baby Jaan interrupted.

'Grrrrr...' Muezza growled. He didn't like being interrupted. Nevertheless he explained, 'It's a transparent surface, made of crystal, under which fish and other water creatures are placed in a pool.'

Baby Jaan's eyes gleamed. 'Clever!' she whispered. 'Very, very clever!'

Queen Bilquis dressed in her best finery and reached the king's royal hall. As she approached him, she saw a pool of water between her and the king. The queen took a deep breath, hoisted up her clothes and stepped 'into' the pool. That was when she realized that it was a sarh.

The queen drew in her breath sharply and dropped her head. She now realized that the king had been demonstrating that without God guiding her, she wouldn't be able to tell the difference between what was real and what was merely a perception.

'I have wronged myself and my people, King Suleiman. I submit to God, who is the lord of mankind, djinns and all that exists,' declared Queen Bilquis.

'So that's the story of the hoopoe, who, too, went to jannat!' Muezza concluded with a flourish.

'What about the king and the queen?' Baby Jaan asked.

'It is said that they married, and that King Suleiman would visit Queen Bilquis in Saba three days a month and return to Jerusalem on his flying carpet. But only God knows . . .' Muezza replied with a smile.

'I love this story!' exclaimed Baby Jaan, sitting with her chin on her knees. 'It has a king and a queen, a hoopoe, a test and a flying carpet! You really are a wonderful storyteller, Muezza.'

Muezza bowed. 'Thank you, thank you . . . I aim to please!'

It's funny, he thought, that listeners liked to hear stories they wanted to hear. Tell them something that made them squirm and they would tell you that you were a bad storyteller.

What is may not be what really is, he told himself and went to sleep.

24

Baby Jaan gazed at the skies as Muezza slept. The stars were out. Distant, cold and sparkling stars that seemed almost at touching distance . . . and try as Baby Jaan did, she didn't think she would ever be able to count them all. Stories were a little like that, she thought. Just when you thought you had come to the end of a story, it led to another one and then another. And Muezza, Baby Jaan thought, was like the sky with a treasure house of starry stories.

I am so lucky to have a friend like him, she thought, moving closer to him so that he would be protected from the desert cold. Then she sat there thinking of all the stories she had been told.

When Muezza opened his eyes, Baby Jaan looked at him and said, '*Finallyyyyy* . . . you're awake! I thought you were going to sleep at least a hundred years.'

Muezza yawned. 'I'm Muezza, Baby Jaan, and not Uzair; that's who slept for a hundred years.'

Baby Jaan leaned forward. 'Who was Uzair? And why did he sleep for a hundred years?'

Muezza smiled. 'Are you curious, or just bored and demanding stories because you have nothing else to do?'

Baby Jaan snorted. 'I think you know the answer to that. Why would I stay here in the desert heat and cold with you, if it wasn't for your stories?'

Muezza shook his head. Yes, he did know the answer. He knew that Baby Jaan was here so he wouldn't be alone. The stories were just the pistachio in the halva.

'Right. Now that we've settled that, draw closer and let me tell you the story of Uzair,' Muezza said, rubbing his paws to revive his blood circulation.

It was freezing cold. Who would have thought the desert could be this . . .
brrrr . . .

Uzair was a wise man who lived his life as God expected him to. In fact, there
was little reason to fault him. One day he was on his way back from inspecting
his properties, and he began to feel hot and tired. It was a scorching day and
all he wanted to do was get away from the heat. Just then, he saw the ruins
of a building. It was wreathed in creepers, and gnarled old trees grew inside
what were once rooms. But it seemed as good a place as any for him to rest
in till the sun went down, he decided. And so he rode his donkey into the
ramshackle courtyard.

The donkey was laden with two baskets—one full of figs and the other
full of grapes. And Uzair was both hungry and thirsty. He retrieved a bowl
from the saddlebag and squeezed the juice of some grapes into it. Then,
soaking the dry bread he had with him in the juice, Uzair ate up. Soon his
belly was full, though there was still some bread and juice left in the bowl.
He started yawning and decided to rest; with his legs propped against a wall,
he lay staring at the ceiling. It was probably the heat or his weariness or a
combination of both, but Uzair saw some bones lying on what used to be a
shelf and reflected. *How can even God bring to life what is dead?*

He hadn't meant to question God's powers, but a doubt is perhaps as
good as a question. And so God sent the Angel of Death to Uzair, who took
his soul away.

Thus Uzair was dead for a hundred years. At the end of a century, God
sent to the ruins an angel to recreate his heart, so he may know; his two eyes,
so he may see. And even as the sentient Uzair was knowing and seeing, the
angel continued to finish what he had begun. He clothed his bones with flesh,
skin and hair. Then he breathed his soul into him. And all the while, Uzair
knew he was being created.

The angel then leaned forward and asked him, 'So how long were
you asleep?'

Uzair shrugged. 'A day or perhaps some part of a day!'

The angel said, 'No, you remained thus for a hundred years! Look at your food and drink.'

Uzair looked at the bowl in which lay the bread soaking in juice; and at the baskets in which the grapes and figs were as fresh as if they had just been plucked.

'Now look at your donkey,' the angel directed. But all Uzair could see was a messy pile of bones that were scattered in all directions.

The angel called to the bones to gather till they formed a skeleton, which he clothed with flesh, skin and hair even as Uzair watched on.

When the angel breathed life into the donkey, it stood up with its ears perked and raised its head to the skies, seeking God's blessings.

Uzair now knew what God had wanted him to see and understand. That here was a sign—himself and the donkey coming back to life was what He had let Uzair witness so he would know God could perform all these miracles.

Uzair mounted his donkey and returned to his village. But everything seemed unfamiliar, and no one was anyone he recognized.

He began looking for his house and finally found it. But how it had changed! Nothing was the way it had been. Uzair swallowed anxiously.

He knocked on the door but there was no response. Uzair wondered where everyone was. He knocked again, with great force, and eventually he heard shuffling steps approach the door. And an old woman, bent, crippled and blind, opened it. Even though her face was lined with a hundred wrinkles, Uzair recognized her. She had been a maiden of only twenty years when he'd left and a servant of the house.

'Is this Uzair's home?' he asked softly.

'Say that again?' she croaked, holding her hand to her ear.

'IS THIS THE HOUSE OF UZAIR?' he bellowed.

'Ah, it is! No need to shout!' she said and burst into tears. 'But there is no one here called Uzair now. A hundred years ago, just on a day like this, he said he would be back by sunset and left . . . and we never saw him again.' Her tears flowed for Uzair had been a gentle and kind master.

'I am Uzair . . .' he said softly. But the old woman wasn't convinced. 'Uzair must surely be dead by now! I don't believe you . . .'

She ran her fingers over his face and touched the donkey's snout as well. 'Your donkey is young . . . and you are, too . . . about forty years of age. You expect me to believe that you are Uzair?' her voice rose in anger.

'As God is my witness, I am Uzair!' he said with finality, hoping that now she would believe him.

'Uzair was a good man, a pious soul. If you are truly Uzair, call on God to help me regain my sight. For only then will I know that you are Uzair if it is you!'

So Uzair asked for God's help and when he touched her eyes, she could see again.

He then took her hand and said, 'Stand up straight.'

And the old maid found that she could! She finally believed that it was none other than her old master, Uzair, except that he looked just as he had on the day he had left a hundred years ago.

Just then, a peculiar keening rose in the desert.

'What is that?' Muezza asked, frightened. He had never heard a wailing like that before.

'It's either the Guls or a sandstorm. Or Guls pretending to be a sandstorm!' Baby Jaan whispered urgently.

'What do we do?' Muezza asked.

'You know that they will sniff me out if they are Guls, don't you? There is just one thing to do. I'm going to turn into a date. Hold me between your

paws. Then hide in the tunnel. And let's pray to God that they don't find us!'

Baby Jaan promptly turned into a date. And Muezza stared at her, flummoxed.

He was on his own.

What was he going to do?

25

Muezza crawled into the tunnel. But he didn't go too far as he didn't want their store of food found and plundered if the approaching party wasn't the Guls. The keening overheard continued, causing Muezza to shiver. He held the date carefully between his paws.

Suddenly the keening stopped, and instead he heard hooves. Muezza felt his intestines drop to his tail. Baby Jaan had described the Guls and he knew for certain that it was them.

The hooves thundered and rumbled above his head. And Muezza saw bits of sand fall into the tunnel. He looked up at the ceiling. Would it cave in, he wondered. He curled into himself and, as an afterthought, hid the date in his mouth.

Suddenly a long claw groped inside the tunnel. Muezza attempted to retreat but it grabbed him by the tail and pulled him out. Muezza stared in shock at what he saw. He had seen nothing like these creatures before. He didn't know if he was among donkeys or goats! For they looked like both.

'What is this? A cat?' one of them shouted.

'If there is a cat, there must be a man or two, or three! And a few rats,' another called out in excitement.

'Oh, good . . . warm human blood and some lovely bones, full of marrow; I don't care much for the meat,' a female Gul said.

'Why don't you eat the cat?' A lean Gul smirked.

'Yikes! *Eat a cat!* I'd rather eat straw. Cat meat is all stringy and the bones are not juicy enough. After all that effort . . .'

'I don't see a man *or* a rat,' an old Gul snorted. 'This one must be a stray!'

'Oh, you know everything, don't you?' an elderly female Gul grunted. 'Old goat!'

'You're an old donkey!' he retorted.

'Let me look at the cat,' the female Gul said. And before Muezza knew it, he was being tossed from one pair of horns to another pair and then to another.

In his head, Muezza went *ouch-ooch-pooch-gooch-tooch-sooch-mooch!* But not a single squeak emerged from his throat.

The female Gul peered at him. 'Cat got your tongue?'

The old male Gul sniggered. 'Do you see another cat around?'

The female Gul stuck her tongue out at the old male one and blew a raspberry. 'And this one's a mangy cat at that! Let's go . . . there's nothing here except for this cat that looks like a rat . . .' she said, tossing him towards a date palm.

Muezza grabbed at the trunk frantically. Nevertheless he collided face-first and hit his nose flat on the tree. And yet, not a sound escaped his mouth.

When the Guls finally left, still keening for no real reason except that they could keen, Muezza climbed up the tree and spat out the date. It landed on the sand and lay there for a while. Then it turned into a white baby camel.

'Muezza!' she called. 'Where are you?'

'Up here,' he said.

Baby Jaan looked up. 'Why don't you come down?'

'My legs are all trembly and my bones hurt . . .' he answered in a feeble voice.

'Come down, Muezza,' Baby Jaan urged. 'Here, jump on to my back!'

Muezza, however, preferred to slither down, and tumbled into a heap at the foot of the tree.

'Thank you, Muezza,' Baby Jaan said. He must be in pain, she realized. The Guls had tossed him around viciously but he hadn't mewed—not even once—in protest or pain.

Muezza nodded but didn't speak.

'When you popped me into your mouth, for a moment I thought, *what is Muezza doing?*' Baby Jaan began.

'You thought you would be unclean because I hid you in my mouth? I'm not dirty. Shahir says that if a cat is clean, you can even drink the water it has drunk!' Muezza sniffed.

'No, Muezza . . . I thought, what if you swallowed me . . .' Baby Jaan sniffed back.

'I guess . . . but what else could I do? I was afraid that they would find you, which is why I concealed you in my mouth. That way, even if you popped out, you would smell of me and they wouldn't know that you were a baby Jaan,' Muezza explained in a weary voice. Even his tail hurt.

Baby Jaan nuzzled Muezza. 'The Guls would have surely hurt me. We are old enemies.'

Muezza only blinked; 'I know', it meant. He was too tired to speak.

'Rest, Muezza,' Baby Jaan advised. 'I will stand guard over you.'

After a while, Muezza woke up from the deep sleep he had fallen into. He stretched slowly and felt much better. His nose still throbbed from the banging against the tree, but he felt less like a tossed-about cat.

Where was Baby Jaan? He looked around and saw her sitting ahead, gazing at the horizon.

'Hello, little one,' he said, walking towards her.

Baby Jaan beamed at him. But he had already spotted the expression of disquiet in her eyes.

'Muezza,' she offered, 'I didn't want to disturb you, which is why I moved away and sat here.'

'Why would you disturb me?'

'Oh,' Baby Jaan sighed. 'I tend to sigh when I'm thinking . . .'

Muezza dropped down to sit beside her. 'What's troubling you?' he asked gently.

Baby Jaan stared at the sand in response. Then in a low voice she asked, 'What if they don't recognize me when I go back home? What if, like in the case of Uzair, they don't believe me when I say I am who I am?'

Muezza took a pawful of sand and trickled it. 'I didn't finish the story of Uzair,' he said.

'Oh, didn't you?' Baby Jaan's mouth fell open. 'I thought it ended when the old maid recognized him!'

'Oh no . . . there's more,' Muezza said and closed his eyes to tell the rest of Uzair's incredible story.

The old maid was so happy upon Uzair's return that she went to the spot where the children of Israel had gathered.

'I come to you with information like you have never known before,' she said, unable to contain her joy and excitement.

'What is it?' they asked in surprise for they could see that she seemed different that day. Uzair's son and grandchildren stared at her.

'My master is back!'

'What is wrong with you?' Uzair's son shook his head in amusement. 'I was always here. I never went away!'

'Not you! But my master Uzair, your father! He is back . . . Master Uzair says God made him die for a hundred years and brought him back to life.'

'And you expect us to believe that?' They laughed loudly.

'I said the same but he called upon God to restore my sight and the strength of my back. Look at me now!' she said, grabbing Uzair's son by his arm. 'Don't you remember what I was like?'

Uzair's son was 118 years old but he remembered that his father had a distinct feature. He looked at the man who stood before him, claiming to be Uzair. The man did look like his father; nevertheless he needed to be certain.

So he declared, 'My father had a black mole between his shoulders.'

Uzair shrugged his robe off his shoulders and everyone could see the black mole! His family was convinced, but the children of Israel still had their doubts. They said, 'Uzair was the only person who knew the entire Torah by heart. Since King Bikhtinassar burnt it, there has been nothing left of it but what little people can recall from memory. So if you are Uzair, as you claim to be, write it all down for us!'

Now Uzair knew that his father, Surukha, had—during the reign of King Bikhtinassar—buried the Torah in a secret place. So he took the children of Israel there, but the scrolls had been eaten away by water and worms. Dismayed, he sat down under a tree that the children of Israel had built a platform around.

It is said that two stars then descended from the heavens and entered his mouth. Thus Uzair remembered everything he had studied of the Torah and was able to begin writing from memory. And so the Torah was recreated and revived by him.

'But Muezza, I don't have a black mole and I know nothing beyond counting up to ten . . .' Baby Jaan moaned in a sad voice.

'Don't worry . . . your family will recognize you. It's not as if you've gone away for a hundred years! Besides, families are like elephants when it comes to remembering things,' Muezza said in a grim voice.

Muezza's siblings still liked to tease him about the time he had gone back to suckling his mother.

Muezza had been attacked by a giant bandicoot. He had never seen one before and thought it was a cat with red, beady eyes. The bandicoot had growled and would have torn him in half if his mother hadn't come to his rescue. He had been badly injured and had taken days to recover. Meanwhile, his mother had had a new litter of kittens. Wounded, Muezza had crawled to her side and she had let him suckle. His mother's milk had healed his bruises and calmed his fears. But his siblings wouldn't let him forget it even though Muezza was a middle-aged cat now. Sometimes, when they wanted to pull him down a peg or two, they called him a baby for it; and every few days, the story of Muezza being nursed when he was no longer a kitten was discussed after a meal, making them all loll around on the grass in splits.

'Elephant? Muezza, what is that?' Baby Jaan asked.

'An incredible beast, Baby Jaan. In fact, a very intelligent creature and super strong!' Muezza declared. He decided he would start a school when he was back with his Shahir. It was nice to be able to share all he knew . . .

'Do you know an elephant story, Muezza? Baby Jaan asked predictably.

'Actually, I do!'

26

The governor of Yemen, Abraha al-Ashram, was looking to consolidate his territories. In order to win the favour of the king of Abyssinia, the Negus, he thought of something new. He decided to build an enormous structure that was meant to be a place of worship. He had been an eccentric man; sometimes cruel, sometimes kind, sometimes wise and sometimes foolish. This time, he wanted the people of Yemen to also know well the extent of his power; so his actions grew extreme. Anyone who came in late for work had his hand cut off. Abraha even stole marble, precious stones and many valuable artefacts from Queen Bilquis's palace for this project. This place of worship was constructed of the finest wood and stone, and everything inside it—the rooftop included—sparkled and gleamed. Lastly he filled it with gold and silver, ebony and ivory, until there was nothing in the world like this edifice.

Then he wrote a letter to the Negus, saying, 'I have built you a shrine like there is no other in the world. You will be its lord and god. In fact, I want to divert all worship from Mecca to Abyssinia.'

When the Arabs heard of the letter sent to the Negus, they were most upset. In fact, one of them was infuriated. In his rage, he went to look at Abraha's edifice. It was just as imposing as he had been led to believe. The incensed man walked around the building and then, in sheer spite, decided to urinate on the walls, making the place dirty and smelly.

No one saw him do so and he got away safely. But the next morning when Abraha went to inspect the building, he saw stains on the walls and caught a nauseating whiff. And he knew that someone had wantonly defiled his shrine. His advisers whispered in his ears, 'It was the Arabs, Your Highness. They are showing you their displeasure for saying that you intend to displace pilgrims from their sacred house to this one you've built for the king of Abyssinia. And so they wanted to make your shrine unworthy of worship!'

Abraha was so angry when he heard this that he clanged together the heads of his advisers, kicked his horse and chopped down a tall tree. Then he ordered the Abyssinians, who were his allies, to help him wage war. In retaliation, he led an expedition. He was going to destroy Mecca, he swore. And anybody or anything that stood in his way would be razed down. For he had what no one else did. An elephant army!

When the Arabs heard of this, they were terrified. But they decided to not take the threat quietly. They would fight him, come what may—the Abyssinian Army, the cavalry or the elephants. A nobleman from among them, called Dhu Nafar, and his clan went to battle against Abraha. But he was defeated. Dhu Nafar was taken prisoner and just as Abraha was giving orders for him to be executed, the prisoner called out, 'Do not kill me! I will be of use to you one day!'

Abraha thought about it and chose to let the prisoner live. Soon the governor of Yemen resumed his journey and reached the land of Khath'am where Nufail ibn Habib al-Khath'ami was waiting with his two clans. Again there was battle and Abraha emerged victorious. And again he decided to execute his prisoner. But Nufail called out, 'Do not kill me! I will be able to guide you to your destination. And you will have my allegiance.'

Abraha was puzzled but intrigued and so he pardoned Nufail, making him his guide.

Soon Abraha was on his way again and came to Taif. There a man came to him with his people and said, 'We are your slaves! We listen and obey, so do not fight us. And our house of worship is not the house you seek. We will send with you someone who can lead you to Mecca!'

So a man called Abu Rughal was asked to direct Abraha and his army to Mecca. And the great expedition proceeded till it reached al-Maghmas, where Abraha sent forth a general called al-Aswad ibn Maqsud with a cavalry unit.

On his mission, the general promptly captured the property of an Arab, which included 200 camels—these were added to Abraha's forces as well. The Arabs decided to fight him at first but the size of Abraha's army made them decide against it.

Next, Abraha sent for one of his faithful servants, called Hanatah al-Himar, and asked him to head to Mecca.

The governor ordered, 'I want you to meet the chief of the land there and tell him that I do not want to wage war against the people. All I want to do is destroy the sacred house of Mecca. We will not harm anyone.' Then, as an afterthought, Abraha added, 'And if the chief decides not to go to battle with us, bring him here to me.'

And so Hanatah reached Mecca and there, when he inquired, he was told that the chief was Abdul Muttalib ibn Hashim. Hanatah went to deliver his message to the chief.

Abdul Muttalib said, 'Of course we have no intention of going to war. This is the sacred house of God, and only He can protect it. Who are we to do it for Him?'

Hanatah was happy to hear this and he ordered Abdul Muttalib to come with him. So Abdul Muttalib, accompanied by his sons, went to Abraha's camp. There Abdul Muttalib met the imprisoned Dhu Nafar, who happened to be a friend of his.

'Can you help me?' Abdul Muttalib asked his friend.

Dhu Nafar shook his head sadly. 'I don't even know if I will be killed—whether it will happen at dawn or dusk. How can I help you, my friend? My word has no value . . .'

'Think! Isn't there anyone you know?' Abdul Muttalib urged gently.

At this, Dhu Nafar's face lit up. 'I know Anis; he is the keeper of the elephants. I can ask him on your behalf and hopefully he can facilitate your meeting with the governor.'

According to plan, Anis chose a moment when Abraha was in a good mood and asked for an audience for Abdul Muttalib. Abraha agreed and soon the appointed day came.

Abdul Muttalib was a very handsome man, with an impressive stature. He stood tall and met the eyes of the governor with neither fear nor arrogance. Abraha was most impressed. The man in front of him seemed an equal. How was he to receive him? Abraha was in a quandary . . .

'So they became best friends!' Baby Jaan's eyes gleamed. 'And the governor gave Abdul Muttalib his elephant!'

'Don't try and second-guess me.' Muezza frowned. 'This isn't *just* a story!'

'It isn't?' Baby Jaan's mouth fell open.

'No, it isn't. So listen and don't interrupt me . . .'

The governor of Yemen, friend of the Abyssinian king, general of an army that can defeat even imagination, wondered what he should do. He knew that if he invited Abdul Muttalib to sit alongside him, the Abyssinians would be offended. But he didn't want to ask the dignified man to sit on the floor, at his feet, either. So Abraha slid on to the rich carpet on the floor and invited Abdul Muttalib to be seated opposite him.

Facing him, Abraha urged the interpreter to ask Abdul Muttalib what he needed. Abraha was startled when he heard the interpreter say that all Muttalib wanted was for his 200 camels, which had been seized, to be returned and nothing else.

'What about the Kaaba? Doesn't he want me to leave that alone?' Abraha asked.

Abdul Muttalib smiled. 'I am the master of my camels and so I need to watch out for them. But the Kaaba has its own Lord to defend it!'

Abraha laughed and agreed.

When Abdul Muttalib returned to his people, he told them what had happened. He asked them to take their belongings and retreat to the mountains. Then Abdul Muttalib, along with a few of his loyal men, stood holding the ring of the Kaaba's door. They invoked God and asked Him to come to their aid when Abraha and his army arrived.

The next morning, Abraha set out for Mecca with his army. He ordered the keeper of the elephant train to direct the animals to trample down the Kaaba. The keeper passed the instruction to Nufail ibn Habib, the appointed guide of the army. That's when Nufail went towards the chief of the elephants, trying not to let his smile show.

The elephant whose name was Mahmoud watched the guide approach and raised his trunk in greeting. He blew gently towards him as if to ask, 'All well?'

Nufail whispered in the elephant's ear, 'Mahmoud, you are in God's sacred land. Kneel down and God will watch over you.'

Mahmoud nodded his head in agreement. He knelt down and refused to budge. The Abyssinians grew furious. For they knew that the other elephants would only do what their leader did. Suddenly it seemed that the elephant army was useless. They forced Mahmoud to stand up but he declined. They beat him on his head but he still wouldn't move. When they directed him towards Yemen, he ran willingly in that direction. When they directed him towards Syria, he gladly ran in that direction, too. Even when they directed him towards the east, he ran towards it happily. But when they made him face Mecca and asked him to run towards the Kaaba to trample the door down, he knelt down again.

That's when God sent some birds from the seaside. Some say the birds had beaks like hawks' and legs like dogs' and were green in colour. Some others say they were black. But it is agreed upon by all that they held in their beak one stone; and in their paws, two. The stones were the size of a chickpea each and were made of clay.

As the birds reached the army, they screamed and rained the stones down on the men. Meanwhile God sent a wind that added ferocity to the rain of stones, and one by one the Abyssinians dropped dead. Soon the land was razed down as if a herd of cattle had eaten up a field of corn, leaving it empty of everything but stalks. Abraha, too, was hit by a stone and his body began to tear up. By evening, his chest had cracked and he'd died.

'So that's the story of the elephant Mahmoud,' Muezza concluded.

Baby Jaan's eyes lit up.

'What are you looking so pleased about?' Muezza asked.

Baby Jaan's voice was full of wonder when she spoke. 'Muezza, I'm glad you told me this story. When I worry of what will come next, I shall remember Mahmoud and how all he needed to know was that God watches over the just and the right.'

27

It was early in the morning but the sun was already blazing hot. Baby Jaan lay in the shade of the date palm; but she wasn't sleepy. She looked at a line of ants crawling their way to wherever it was they were going. Suddenly her thoughts went awhirl, like a sandstorm, and settled down to becoming a single thought that was as big as Mahmoud, the blessed elephant. She looked at Muezza, who was making little cat snores as he slept. She didn't want to annoy him by waking him up. But the thought was sitting inside her head and nudging her to be let out. Eventually she could bear it no longer.

She cleared her throat gently. But Muezza continued to snore. So Baby Jaan produced a snore-like sound, hoping that it would wake him up.

It did. Muezza yowled and ran up the tree.

'What's wrong, Muezza?' Baby Jaan called out flabbergasted by his strange behaviour. Muezza peered from between the leaves.

'Did you hear that growl? It sounded like a lion!'

Baby Jaan wanted to giggle. She didn't dare tell him that she had only tried to snore like him.

'I think you must have imagined it . . . I don't see any lion lurking here . . .' she said airily. 'I see some ants . . . nothing but them.'

Muezza came down the tree, looking puzzled. 'Do you think I dreamt it?'

'Quite likely,' said Baby Jaan and, seizing the opportunity, added, 'Speaking of ants . . .'

Muezza darted a suspicious look at her. 'Who said anything about ants? Y-you did . . . not me!'

'Does it matter who is speaking of ants? My question is, does God only bless the big and beautiful animals and birds?'

'Why do you ask that?' Muezza frowned.

'The whale and the elephant, the cow, the ram and the heifer, the dog and the donkey, the hoopoe and the camel . . . I don't hear about the scarab or the butterfly or the ant going to jannat!'

There! The thought that had been eating away at Baby Jaan popped out in a torrent of words.

'Hmm . . .' Muezza said thoughtfully. 'It *does* seem like that, doesn't it?'

'*Yessss!*' Baby Jaan nodded furiously.

'Well, then, you're wrong, Baby Jaan! God doesn't judge by size or colour or beauty . . . In fact, I'm going to tell you about the blessed ant!'

'*An ant!*' Baby Jaan's mouth fell open. 'How can that be?'

'Why not? Do you remember King Suleiman?'

'Yes, the hero of my favourite story!' Baby Jaan grinned happily.

'Good. This happened during King Suleiman's time . . .'

The beautiful land of Palestine had been struck by a terrible famine. The rains hadn't arrived and the rivers had run dry; the crops had failed and everywhere people were running helter-skelter, looking for food. When even the granaries were empty and there were no animals left to cook and eat, the hungry folk plucked the leaves off trees. And when those, too, were eaten, they ate blades of grass. Soon there was nothing left to eat.

King Suleiman called his people and said, 'Follow me to the desert. We shall beseech God to forgive us for our sins and perhaps then the rains will come!'

As they walked, King Suleiman saw an ant standing on its two legs, raising its hands up towards the sky. He paused, amazed at what the ant was doing. Now as King Suleiman knew the language of all birds, animals and insects, he listened to what the ant was saying in its reedy voice.

'O God! We may be the smallest of your creatures and we cannot survive unless you make it possible for us to. And we have done nothing wrong, as you know. We, unlike other animals, lift burdens that are twice our own weight. When we find a store of grains, we tell each other so that all may share and all may eat. So please do not punish us for the sins of human beings. Please send down the rains so that the trees can grow and the fields can become green! Only if there is grain will we have food to eat.'

King Suleiman clapped his hands and asked his people to stop. 'There is no need for us to go any further. The prayer of this ant is enough!'

And the skies did darken as the clouds gathered, and soon a drop fell. Then the heavens opened up and the rain came down in thick sheets, filling the wells and the rivers, and turning everything green and beautiful.

Baby Jaan nodded happily. 'I'm so glad. I really love the stories about King Suleiman! So, this ant went to jannat?'

Muezza smiled. 'Actually, no. That's another ant.'

Once King Suleiman was travelling through his kingdom with a big group of men, djinns and birds. Soon they reached a valley of ants. When the chief of the ants saw the pomp and glory with which the king and his entourage were approaching, he called out to his colony, 'Go into your holes. Run, run, run! Or we may be trampled and crushed by the approaching men and djinns.' Then he waited, making sure everyone was safely hidden.

King Suleiman smiled at this warning sounded by the ant chief, and ordered his retinue to wait till the ants went inside their holes. 'None of us should hurt any ant while passing over their land,' he commanded.

When each one of the ants had retreated inside their holes, King Suleiman knelt on the ground and spoke to the chief of the ants. 'You are brave but my people wouldn't have hurt you or your fellow ants! Don't you know that I am a messenger of God and would never cause you harm?'

The chief replied, 'O messenger of God! I wasn't afraid for my ants. We are small creatures that no one notices. But we notice everything, and I didn't want my colony to forget the glory of God after seeing your magnificence.'

King Suleiman listened to the chief of the ants and understood what he was being told even if it was conveyed gently. It is said that the king renounced his ostentatious displays thereafter, lived humbly and became prudent.

'What do you think?' Muezza asked Baby Jaan. 'Which is your favourite among the blessed animals? And don't say it's the she-camel. You're not really a camel, you know!'

Baby Jaan shook her head. 'I can't decide. I like them all!'

Muezza looked at the horizon. It was going to be almost four days—but where was his Shahir? He was beginning to lose hope. Baby Jaan and he couldn't live here like this forever . . . the food would soon run out and the army of Jaans would be back—if not tomorrow then certainly the day after.

Baby Jaan was humming under her breath. 'Muezza,' she said suddenly, 'it's been a while since I tried shape-shifting. Who should I try and become now? An elephant or a bird from the seaside?'

Muezza was struck by a thought. 'If you become a bird, you can fly far ahead and see if anyone's coming our way!'

'Then bird I shall be! A hawk whose eyes can see far, far ahead . . .' Baby Jaan said and rose up in the air as a hawk.

When Baby Jaan returned, she shook her head sadly. 'I didn't see anyone or anything.'

Muezza's face fell. But he didn't say anything.

'Don't be afraid, Muezza. It's just a matter of time. Anyway, I will soar across the skies once again, but, in the meanwhile, tell me something . . . how did your Shahir come to know all of this?'

Muezza rested his chin on a little rock. 'I used to wonder the same till I heard it being narrated. The story of Shahir is an unusual one, too.'

28

Shahir's real name is Muhammad. His father, Abdullah ibn Abdul-Muttalib, died even before he was born. And his mother, Amina Bint Wahb, passed away when he was six years old. He was brought up by his grandfather, Abdul-Muttalib, who died two years later, when he was eight. Thereafter he was looked after by his uncle, Abu Talib. I don't know much about those years except that Shahir managed as well as he could. He didn't learn to read or write but he was apprenticed to a merchant and soon came to be well regarded.

Around this time, Khadija, a rich widow and merchant of the Quraysh tribe, was looking for someone she could send with her caravan to oversee business matters. Khadija's caravan was so extensive that it equalled the sum of all the caravans of the rest of her tribe. Naturally she needed someone very trustworthy.

Khadija was widely known as a sound businesswoman. But she did not travel with her caravan as it wasn't safe for a noblewoman to undertake the long summer journey to Syria or the winter journey to Yemen. Instead she employed others to trade on her behalf for a commission.

That year Khadija needed an agent to conduct a transaction in Syria, and someone recommended Shahir for the job. Though he was young, only twenty-five years old, the experience he had gained from working with his uncle had made him quite sought after. He was known to be both honest and honourable, and so she offered him double the usual commission.

Khadija also sent one of her servants, Maysarah, to assist him. On his return, Maysarah wouldn't stop talking about Shahir, exclaiming that he was honourable, he was noble, he was kind. Khadija was impressed, especially as he had brought back twice as much profit as she had expected.

Maysarah had something even more important to say. 'Mistress,' he started, unable to hide the awe he felt, 'on our way back, we stopped to rest under a tree. Soon Muhammad fell asleep. That's when I noticed two angels standing above him, weaving a cloud to protect him from the sun's blistering heat. As if that wasn't enough, a monk passing that way said that only a prophet could rest under that tree. I tell you, he is not just any other man!'

Khadija was both intrigued and afraid by what she heard. Meanwhile, she had a strange dream—she saw the sun descend from the sky into her courtyard, lighting up her home in a golden glow. And so she went to meet her cousin Waraqah ibn Nawfal, telling him what her servant had claimed as having seen, as well the strange dream she'd had.

Her cousin tugged at his beard, deep in thought. 'If what your servant said is true, then Muhammad must be the prophet we have been waiting for!'

'But what was the meaning of my dream? And why me?' Khadija asked in a frightened voice.

Waraqah smiled at her, amused by her fear. She was a rich woman but she wasn't a hard-hearted merchant who only counted her coins. She didn't believe in any god except mercy and truth. So she fed and clothed the poor, and helped her relatives. 'Do not be alarmed, for it means that the prophet will grace your home!'

That was when Khadija considered proposing marriage to Shahir. Until then, many wealthy Quraysh men had already asked for her hand in marriage but she had refused every one of them. So Khadija sent her friend Nafisa to ask Shahir if he would consider marrying her. And Nafisa went about it delicately.

'A young man like you needs a wife,' she began.

Shahir was hesitant. 'I would like to marry but I have no money to support a wife.'

Nafisa then said, 'There is a woman I know who is capable of supporting herself. Would you consider it then?'

So Shahir agreed to meet with Khadija, after which they consulted their respective uncles. The uncles, too, agreed to the marriage.

The years passed. Shahir was no longer a young man, and he increasingly felt distressed by what was happening around him. Earlier he had been buffeted by life and its ups and downs; and he'd had no time to consider the many evils of the world. But now that he was older, he could no longer remain oblivious to the injustice and prejudices of society.

And there was another matter. The people of Mecca claimed descent from Ibrahim through Ismail and, together, they revered the shrine at the Kaaba. But over the years, some among them had begun worshipping idols. However, there were some others who were disgusted by this practice and wanted to return to the religion of Ibrahim and what it had stood for; they sought the truth about God through their inner consciousness. And Shahir was one among them. It made him wonder about God and why God had chosen to create a world which was the way it was. Shahir began to spend a great deal of time on his own, pondering about this and wondering how divine guidance would come his way to set the world aright.

Once a year, in the month of Ramadan—the month of heat—Shahir began to retreat to a cave called Mount Hira, two miles away from Mecca, for solitary contemplation and reflection. It was on a night towards the end of that quiet month that his first revelation came to him. The year was 610 CE and Shahir was almost forty years old at the time.

Shahir was in deep meditation when he heard a voice. 'Read.'

He replied, 'I cannot read.'

The voice spoke louder, '*Read!*'

Shahir answered again, '*I cannot read!*'

The third time, the voice thundered as it commanded, 'READ!'

Now Shahir asked, 'What shall I read?'

The voice recited,

> Read: In the name of thy Lord who
> createth,
> Createth man from a clot.
> Read: And it is thy Lord, the most
> bountiful,
> Who teacheth by pen,
> Teacheth man that which he
> knew not!

Shahir felt as though the words had been inscribed upon his heart. He went out of the cave and heard that awe-inspiring voice speak again, 'O Muhammad, thou art God's messenger and I am Jibril.'

Saying so, the archangel appeared before him. Shahir was blinded by a bright light and tried to turn away; but whichever way he turned, the angel stood before him.

Shahir returned to Khadija, worried and frightened. Khadija, however, reassured him that God would not let anything hurt him and that it had to have been a sign from God—he had been chosen to be the prophet.

Shahir soon began preaching to his family and friends, while the people of Mecca began to suspect that he had gone a little mad. The first of his converts was his wife Khadija, the second was his cousin Ali Talib—whom he had adopted—and the third, his companion Zaid, a former slave. Thus Shahir's initial converts were humble, simple people; and slowly the numbers grew.

It is said that over the next twenty-three years after the first revelation, the archangel Jibril continued to reveal God's word to Shahir. And Shahir told his followers to write it all down.

'Shahir takes me everywhere he goes. And so I hear him preach, Baby Jaan. That's how I know the stories even if I may not understand them fully,' Muezza said.

'I think you understand what I understood, too. That God watches over us. That we are all God's creations. We may be different . . . but that's just how we look, when, in fact, we are all the same,' Baby Jaan said carefully.

Muezza nodded. It occurred to him then that his stories had not been empty words. Baby Jaan had understood what the true message of God had been all about. In some strange way, it comforted Muezza as well. He, too, would have to trust in God. His Shahir *would* return for him.

Baby Jaan stood up. 'And now I must fly to the skies again.'

Muezza gazed at the hawk soaring into the clouds. He felt quite dizzy even watching her. The hawk was gone a long while. Then it came back, circling the skies and swooping towards him.

'Muezza!' exclaimed Baby Jaan. 'They are on their way towards you!'

'How do you know it's my Shahir?' Muezza asked, quite sure that Baby Jaan had made a mistake.

'I heard them speak and I heard a man tell another that Shahir was very upset that you had been left behind. Your Shahir himself is on his way to fetch you!'

'So I guess it's time to say *Khuda hafiz* . . .' Muezza bowed and it suddenly struck them both that they may never see each other again. Baby Jaan's lower lip trembled. Muezza felt a lump in his throat.

'I have to signal your people to come fetch you, too,' he said brusquely. Baby Jaan nodded.

Quickly, Muezza went down to the food cellar where he had hidden the magic whistle. He fetched it and, standing alongside Baby Jaan, he blew the instrument.

And as they watched—the cat and the baby djinn—an army of white camels filled the horizon.

'Will we ever meet again?' Baby Jaan asked wistfully.

'God willing . . .' Muezza replied softly.

'God *will* be willing. But we must be, too!' Baby Jaan said tenderly.

Muezza rubbed his head against hers. 'Yes, little one . . . we will.'

And just as the Jaan army drew closer, Muezza said, 'Hey, Baby Jaan, I have to tell you something . . . I can't read minds—you mutter everything you think. So I just read your lips!'

Baby Jaan grinned. Even as Muezza watched, the army was upon them and had whisked Baby Jaan away. And from the other side of the desert, there came men on horses.

His Shahir was here.

Glossary

◈ Djinn: In Arabian lore, djinns are supernatural spirits—of a high order of intelligent beings, but lower in rank than angels—who assume human or animal form and intervene in the affairs of men.

◈ Houris: Alluring, doe-eyed maidens of fair skin, houris are the celestial, pure companions who greet believers in jannat.

◈ Sahabahs: Companions of Prophet Muhammad, and followers and propagators of his Islamic tenets, sahabahs attested to the life and teachings of the prophet, which formed the foundations of the Islamic way of life.

◈ Al-Zuhra: The planet Venus, Zuhra is a common Muslim name, meaning 'the radiant one', and is one of the titles conferred on Prophet Muhammad's daughter Fatimah for her beauty and virtue.

◈ Day of Resurrection or Day of Judgement: Significant events that are to occur at the end of time and after the death of all creation, when only God remains, this is when God will resurrect all creatures. Then He will serve judgement on all actions such that the faithful and the devoted will be rewarded for their deeds. That will mark the beginning of the hereafter, an everlasting afterlife.

◈ Kaaba: The cube-shaped stone building in the centre of Islam's most sacred mosque, Al-Masjid al-Haram, in Mecca, Saudi Arabia, the Kaaba marks the holy spot in whose direction believers must turn to when they pray from wherever they are in the world. The direction of the Kaaba is called the qiblah.

◈ Mecca: The holiest city for Muslims, Mecca is located in a desert valley in Saudi Arabia. It is the birthplace of Prophet Muhammad and of Islam itself. The annual pilgrimage to Mecca, which all able believers must undertake at least once in their lifetime, is called the hajj.

Keffiyeh: Usually donned by Arabs, the keffiyeh is a traditional headdress in the form of a square, chequered scarf tied with a band. It provides protection against the sun and the sand in desert regions.

Attar: A natural perfume, attar is a fragrant oil extracted from flowers, fruits, herbs or spices, after which it is distilled, aged and then bottled for use.

Bedouin: An individual of a group of nomadic Arabs who roam the desert.

Prophets and Messengers of God: A messenger of God—a Rasul—receives a revelation from God and thus delivers a new law, whereas a prophet—a Nabi—is sent by God to propagate His existing tenets. So while all Rasuls are Nabis, not all Nabis are Rasuls.

Haram: That which is forbidden by God and Islamic law, all acts haram and their prohibition form the moral centre of Islamic belief. Haram comprises sacred things being kept away from the impure, as well as sinful acts that are never to be committed.

Children of Israel or the Banu Israel people: Descendants of Israel, which is another name for Prophet Yaqub, the children of Israel were actually the twelve sons of Yaqub who swore to follow their father's faith. Prophet Yaqub preached the word of God as his forefather Ibrahim had.

Torah: The word of God revealed to Prophet Musa, the Torah is a holy book in Islam.

Khuda Hafiz: A parting greeting, 'Khuda hafiz' literally translates to 'May God protect you'.

Selected Bibliography

This list is by no means a complete record of all the works and sources that have been consulted, but only those that have helped shape this book in particular.

Books

Kathir, Ibn. *Stories of the Prophets*. Translated by Muhammad Mustapha Geme'ah, Al-Azhar. Darussalam, 2000.

———*Stories of the Quran*. Translated by Ali As-Sayed Al-Halawani. Dar Al-Manarah, n.d.

Pickthall, Marmaduke William. *The Meaning of the Glorious Quran*. World Islamic Publications, 1999.

Online Resources[*]

https://groups.google.com/forum/#!msg/naqshbandi/G9zcx1t235w/ZVzCxfIRajkJ

http://www.angelfire.com/on/ummiby1/companions2.html

http://www.iqraonline.net/8-famous-mountains-caves-referenced-in-islamic-history/

http://www.djinnuniverse.com/a-short-course-on-the-djinn

http://www.theonlyquran.com/99names.php

http://www.theislamicemailcircle.com/discover/history-of-prophet-ibrahim-alaihissalaam-2/

[*]Content and URL may have changed since last accessed.

Acknowledgements

It takes a publisher of rare courage to invest in a book that many others, in all probability, would shy away from. In Hemali Sodhi I found not just a fearless person, who understood the significance of this book, but also a child's heart who fell in love with the two protagonists, Muezza the cat and Baby Jaan the camel. Does any writer need more?

Thanks are also due to Sohini Mitra for nudging me back on to the road each time I swerved away; to Harshad Marathe, Gunjan Ahlawat and Meena Rajasekaran for making the stories come alive; and to Kankana Basu for painstakingly fact-checking them and for her careful copy-editing.

And, as always, I couldn't have done this without my parents, Bhaskaran and Soumini, who taught me the true joy of stories—the telling and the listening—and what they can achieve.

And to the countless feral cats that have made my garden their home for as long as they have lived, and have given me much delight—notably Vicki, Cristina, Barcelona, Swathithirunaal, Thyagaraja, Muthuswamy, Shyama, Musa, Bua, Ginger, Ivan, Coonie and Muffin—'Salaam, salaam'.